At the Center of it All
…A Love Story

Tierza M .Groce

At the Center of it All…A Love Story

Tierza M Groce

Copyright © 2016 Executive Grind Publishing

Scripture quotations, unless otherwise noted are taken from THE HOLY BIBLE, NEW LIVING TRANSLATION, TOUCHPOINT BIBLE EDITION Copyright © 1996

ISBN: 978-0692758434
ISBN-13: 0692758437

Executive Grind Publishing
www.Executivegrind.com
www.TierzaSpeaks.com

Editorial Services by Shawn Jackson

Printed in the Unites States of America
First Edition 2016

I dedicate this book to Bennie Marie, my Nana Bear – thank for never simply wiping my tears and telling me everything will be ok but telling me to choose wisely my reaction to things that come against me in this world and to never forget I have a choice. I appreciate truth because of your unwillingness to lie and can boldly dismiss fear because you walked fearless in faith before me.

CONTENTS

Acknowledgments   i

1 Caramel Macchiato   3

2 Blocking   17

3 Truth Be Told   31

4 Until Next Time   49

5 From the Top   67

6 Rolling the Dice   83

7 Uncovered   97

8 Yes   109

9 Changes   121

10 Everything Happens for a Reason   137

11 At the Center of it All   151

About the Author   169

ACKNOWLEDGMENTS

To my heavenly father…your word says ask and it shall be given. I asked to be used by you to bring positive change to all I come in contact with; you gave me a ministry that by your power will reach those in need of just what the words on these pages have to offer.

To my mother…for changing your life and allowing me to have my best chance at being the star you always said I was.

To my godmother (R.I.H.)…for placing in my little 14 year old hands *I Know Why the Caged Bird Sings* and cutting a window into the box of my life allowing me to see a world I may have never otherwise been exposed to.

To Sawanda…for showing me that being me was good enough by simply allowing me to be just that all the time; you never questioned and you never judged…instead encouraged and ministered to my heart in my broken moments.

To my son…for your big heart and silliness that lifts my spirits and gives the push I need when I am feeling low. Mommy loves you!

To Sasha…for believing in my gift before even knowing much of the person I am. I truly believe we were positioned by God to meet.

To Moneesha…for gifting me with the notebook that sparked the writer in me to surface and write again just when I thought I had nothing else to write about.

To Justin…for putting a mirror before me and encouraging me to fall in love with all that is me so that I can give my whole self to all that lies before me. I appreciate all that you have put into making my dreams come true.

i

CHAPTER 1

CARAMEL MACCHIATO

AT THE CENTER OF IT ALL...A LOVE STORY

CARAMEL MACCHIATO

It's the holiday season and more people are out than usual. The Salvation Army bells are ringing for donations, children's eyes glowing and adults staring, hopeful, at the great gifts behind the windows at the major department stores. Lights of red and green and grand Christmas trees dress the city.

Making her way down to Center Coffee Shop in the heart of the city, Gabby smiles and inhales the holiday joy all around her.

"Tall Caramel Macchiato?"

The young lady calls out to be claimed. Approaching the counter, two hands reach for one cup.

"…been waiting about 10 minutes and, during that wait, you just now appeared. Maybe yours is next, but great choice."

Gabby nods and wishes a good day to the man whose hand is still extended towards the now empty-handed employee who had called out the order. She gives an 'I'm sorry' smile and goes on with her job.

Clearing his throat and straightening his tie, the empty handed man speaks to Gabby's back as she heads for the door.

"Yes, it is a great choice. I order it every Saturday at noon but, in all the years of me coming and placing the same order, you just now appear." Not once turning around Gabby smiles and continues out the doors of the coffee shop. Once out she is tempted to look through the glass but instead makes a mental note of his every Saturday caffeine fix confession.

By Wednesday Gabby finds herself completely consumed with thoughts of the man at the coffee shop and what he looked like.

"I think he was tall because when I looked at him I looked up. Yeah, he's tall. Oooh, and chocolate! Not dark chocolate but that nice milk chocolate. Remember, John who was on the praise team at church? Think of him, just way more handsome and professional looking."

Gabby had been on the phone for over 30 minutes going on and on about what she thought the man at the coffee shop looked like. Tasha, her friend of 15 years, whom she met while working at a major mall back home in the Midwest during high school, was kindly but barely listening.

"Ok, Gab...stop! Just check him out again this coming Saturday. If he's all that you remember him to be then talk to him; you're far from shy." She reminds her longtime friend before getting off the phone to shower and go to sleep.

Gabby lays in bed wondering if she should show up at the coffee shop on Saturday and, if she did, how would he view her: insane, lonely...desperate?

Oh no, she thought, *I can't be desperate*!

The rest of the week Gabby throws herself into her work. The editing company she has been with for 4 years has sentenced her to a vacation. This is considered a prison sentence for Gabby because her life is her work; she is rather dysfunctional and unorganized without it.

Fri-day was quickly turning into Fri-night. After wrapping up an editing job for a new show to air on a major network, Gabby gathers her belongings from her office as she won't see it for the next two weeks.

"Enjoy your vacation, wish it was me," said Saundra, a newbie to the company peeks her head into Gabby's office. Gabby looks up quickly, removing the free falling natural curl from her eyes, she smiles and nods at her.

"Two weeks will fly by faster than you think. I'll be back soon." Gabby tells her.

Saundra, still standing in the doorway seemingly with something more to say begins to annoy Gabby. This was the first time Gabby has ever shared more than good morning in speaking with the new employee and Saundra had a way with others around the office, as though she was familiar with them. Gabby wants no part of that.

"I am heading out; enjoy your holiday as well." Gabby nods again at Saundra who finally gets the idea and excuses herself.

As she reaches over to turn the light off at the door of her office she glances over at the calendar on the wall, tomorrow was Saturday. She had circled it with a blue highlighter.

Feeling silly about doing that, she turns off the light and decides at that moment not to show up tomorrow afternoon.

VACATION

Week one of Gabby's vacation was well planned out way before the date. She would enjoy a spa day, go ice skating and snow tubing up in the mountains. Verna being the most adventurous of the friends did all of the planning. Tasha's aunt lives near the mountain resort, so they were able to spend above and beyond on drinks, food and activities as lodging was not an expense. Terri, Tasha's aunt, has a youthful spirit but her body was not on the same page as her spirit. At only 46 she has had two knee surgeries, a hip replacement and even a cancer scare.

"You know I would love to hit them slopes with you ladies, but I have so much to do, maybe next time though." Her denial speaks.

"Yeah Aunt Terri, next time for sure," Tasha encourages.

On the final week of vacation, Gabby buys, wraps and ships Christmas gifts to her mother and younger brother. A new sweater for her brother and a fabulous piece of jewelry for her mother always did the trick.

Christmas shopping for the family brings her to a moment of sadness remembering that she doesn't have a relationship with her older sister, therefore, not sending her a gift. Gabby did however, make it a point to send her a card every holiday, regardless of the fact she never returned the kindness or even text a thank you.

Gabby often fantasizes about regaining that relationship with her sister. After years of a non-existent relationship though, she believes there is no chance.

Christmas day arrives and, being that it's her first Christmas not celebrated with family, she spends most of the day on speaker phone with her mother while preparing her version of Christmas dinner: Baked chicken wings, collard greens, corn bread and baked macaroni and cheese.

"You should have ordered a ham from Honey Bake baby. Baked chicken is a regular weeknight meal. I know I taught you better." Gabby laughs at her mother's choice of words. She had her father to thank for the little she *did* know about cooking .

As quickly as it came, it left. Christmas now over Gabby does some winter cleaning and organizing of her apartment. She puts away the Christmas tree and removes all the cards from the mantel and lays to rest the issues of the past year.

"A new year, a new start!" She professes as she places the top over her ornament box and stores it in the hallway closet until next year.

REVERSE

There is no blowing of horns or cheers made with Champagne. Gabby even dismisses the countdown to midnight.

A kiss to the photo of her father next to her bed and a prayer for a clean heart brings her into the New Year where she wakes up fresh and ready to jump into it and back to her work routine.

Opening the door to her office she gasps! There was a stench that was so strong she was convinced something had died in there while she was on vacation.

"Victor!" She says in a low but firm voice, storming into the office directly to the right of hers. "Something has died in my office. I can't go in there until I know what, when and that it's been removed."

Chuckling, Victor, who she reports to, pushes away from his mahogany brown desk and lifts all 300lbs of himself up from the leather seat made specially to hold a person of his size.

"Did you go away a woman and come back a little girl?" He waddles toward her, waving his arm for her to move aside. As he enters her office he too agrees that something has died in there. Feeling his breakfast beginning to come up he quickly closes the door and suggests she sit at the cubicle across from her office to get started and he would call pest control to have her office looked at.

Gabby throws her purse on the desk of the 25 sq. foot space with cloth walls and an overhead shelf. Plopping down in the uncomfortable blue cloth chair she sighs in disbelief.

How did I end up back here...square one! She questions.

As she attempts to adjust to her temporary workspace she begins to wonder about her life outside of this cubicle; the life outside this office. Though she was raised in a two-parent home she had the support of a one-parent home growing up. Her mother never really had time for encouraging words and pep talks because she was too focused on achieving her own goals. Gabby didn't hate her mother because she was going after more but she did grow away from her because there was never really time to make a connection. Her father, George, was at every softball game, every spelling bee and even chaperoned field trips and dances. He dried her tears and bandaged her scars.

Reflecting on her childhood opened wounds she thought had long before healed. A pain set in her gut and a longing in her heart for her father who passed away a week before her High School graduation.

Sitting in her old chair, within the confines of her old cubicle, she thinks of all the people she frowned on and considered less than because this was their workspace. Not once did she think about their journey to that space or how it may just be a stepping stone to the next thing for them. She never thought about their support system, or lack thereof.

All she knew was that the people who occupied these cubicles were her age and should have been doing more with their lives, in her opinion.

Gabby leans back in the uncomfortable chair looking at her closed office door. She wonders if she is deserving of the office space that is currently reeking of death on the other side of it.

Maybe there's no rodent at all. Maybe I'm the stench that needs to be removed from that office.

She wonders and reflects on into the afternoon. But shortly after consuming her tuna melt and sweet potato fries, all was well in her soul regarding her current place in life. While flipping through a magazine during lunch she read:

"God has given all of us the capacity to make good choices when it comes to our lives...don't be so passive with your life decisions."

By day's end she was still not granted access into her office. Hopeful to be back into the space she worked so hard to have by morning, she skips out of the office straight to the flower shop at the corner of her home to grab a plant to place on her desk when she returns in the morning.

STEPPING OUT

"I know you hate going out but you love jazz music. So, I was thinking..."

As Verna, Gabby's college friend who taught her all about the birds, bees and mosquitoes, paused for reaction, Gabby contemplated hanging up the phone.

"Don't think too hard. You know I am not going into the city on a week night. Some of us have to work real jobs that require a full night's sleep."

Verna was a photographer and did very well for herself publishing her pictures in major magazines. She also ran a small side business creating greeting cards and unique invitations.

"The decent men come out on weeknights...we both could stand to meet someone new. Besides, Tasha works the box office. We can get in the event free," Verna continued.

Gabby was now convinced. Not because she needed a hand-out but because it would be nice to see what's out there as far as potential men. She never went out with any intentions to pick up men though. She left that up to her girls, mainly Verna.

After a quick brush to her cheeks of Dior's Rose blush and stroke to her lashes with Maybelline's high volume mascara, Gabby is ready to step out. About an hour into rummaging through her closet she finally settled for a simple navy blue dress that was fitted to her slim waist line, pleating at her full hips and flowing loosely thereafter stopping just above her knees hiding her thick thighs. Silver accessories and a little camel colored clutch completed her Monday night look.

Gabby arrives at Verna's house promptly at seven so they can ride together in Verna's new pearl white two seated BMW sport car.

"I got a great deal on it." Verna lied when she shared the news of her new car with her friends.

Everything a worldly single successful woman would want, Verna has unapologetically. Including a gorgeous loft style home furnished with all white everything, a fridge filled with yogurt and bottled water, and a new man occupied the bachelorette pad every other day.

Gabby admired Verna's taste in home style but would never admit it aloud. She figured that would be too close to admitting she was like Verna in a minor, yet factual, way.

Before Gabby could ring the buzzer Verna was twisting the knob.

Much like Gabby, Verna is very full figured. She's dressed in an all-black leather one piece jumper that fit so tight breathing couldn't have been an option.

Shaking her head Gabby asks, "Oh, is that all you could find for an evening out during the week? It's Jazz, Verna, not an audition for a hip-hop video."

Laughter fills the night air as the ladies go on to enjoy their evening.

When they arrive to the box office, Tasha is already sitting on the opposite side of the glass grinning from ear to ear.

"The show doesn't start for another hour, sit with me! Come through the side door," she directs them.

JOSIAH

On the other side of town, Josiah stands outside waiting for Janay, his date for the evening. He had spent his day in meetings and at the gym so, at nightfall, he was ready to go relax and have a good time.

He has known Janay for about three years now and she was often his date when he wanted to hang out. She fit the description of the woman people expected to see a man like him with: very attractive, sexy and sophisticated. She was tall and slim with a perfect, beautiful smile; a college graduate with no children and a rather prestigious family line.

Having her on his arm complemented his outward appearance more than his inward.

As she walks toward him he doesn't pay attention to her slim, size four, frame or the short red dress that fit that frame perfectly. What did attract his attention was her hair; he loved her full shoulder length hair that was always shining and full of body.

"Where to tonight," Janay asks while climbing into the car. Josiah smiles as he closes the door to the black Mercedes he was holding open for her.

"Hope you're in the mood for jazz." He plants a gentle kiss on her cheek, places his hand on her thigh and turns out into the flow of traffic. Silence fills the car as the pair rides along to the club as conversation wasn't one of Janay's best features. Words would come out but often fall on Josiah's uninterested ears.

Inside the club Gabby, Verna and Tasha are being swooned by Valdez, the owner. Tasha, has a 'friends with benefits' relationship with him by her choice. If it were up to Valdez, he would have married her by now and impregnated her with at least two kids.

Three strong drinks and 4 weak pick-up lines later, Verna was ready to go. They made it midway through the second set and this was reason to be proud. Verna usually was picked up by a handsome professional man about an hour in and she's out the door leaving her dear friends behind.

"Well Tash, you know that means I am out too; Verna is my ride." Gabby, who had only a glass of wine, was putting on her jacket when she noticed coming toward her a familiar face.

"I am running to the little girl's room."

Gabby hurries away to give herself a good look over in the mirror just in case it was really her vision and not the wine seeing that familiar face.

Every natural curl in place, teeth pearly white and dress neatly lying over her body she was ready to take a second look. She walks out of the restroom and right into her second look. They met chest to face.

"Excuse me, Ms. Caramel Macchiato." Josiah grins.

"No, excuse me." Gabby insists while staring surprised at the man whom, to her delight, looks more attractive than she remembers.

"It appears you were about to walk into the ladies room...you need to go further down the hall where you will find the men's room. Unless I am mistaken," she asks while her eyes find their way to the man's bulge.

She attempts to make her way around the wall of a man but he gently grabs at her wrist.

"Josiah...Josiah Emmit."

Pulling her left arm away she extends her right suggesting a handshake.

"Caramel...Caramel Macchiato; but you already knew that."

Josiah accepts her suggestion and they share a laugh. A brief silence fell between them. Gabby, thinking to herself she needs to get back to her girls before they come looking for her and embarrass her. Josiah thinking, he has been standing at the door of the bathroom waiting for Ms. Macchiato so long, Janay must be wondering where he is.

Reaching into her clutch, Gabby finds a business card. She always tries to keep one or two on her no matter where she is, every outing is an opportunity to network she believes.

"Call me."

Unintentionally, Josiah doesn't get around to calling Gabby for a couple of days. Finally making the call he attempts to apologize and explain why it had taken so long. This was all so shocking for Gabby because she thought getting a call this soon was actually pretty good. Enjoying his belief of disappointment she let him go on, playing into it throughout the conversation.

"No worries, I have a life too, you know." She said, finally giving him the feeling she was letting him off the hook when in reality she never had him on it.

GETTING TO KNOW

As exciting as a first date was, it was also nerve wracking. Gabby does all she can to prepare for the date, nails, eyebrow wax, fresh twist out and facial but she feels she was missing something even after all of that.

"You got some condoms," Verna asks jokingly as they leave the hair salon. Though confident that was not what she was missing, she parted ways with Verna no longer questioning what she was forgetting but what she had already forgotten. Verna's condom question reminded Gabby that she was abstaining from sex and has been for many years.

Josiah promptly arrives in front of the convenience store at the end of Gabby's block at six o'clock as agreed. She stands there in her one and only little black dress and black heels. She is kept warm by her checkered pea coat and red scarf. Josiah jumps out to open the door for her. She pauses to admire his style. Dressed in gray slacks, black button up, black dress shoes and black and grey striped scarf, their looks certainly complemented each other.

Gabby had agreed to dinner at a popular steakhouse in the city even though she didn't really care for steak. She and Verna had reviewed the menu while getting pedicures earlier and she mentally noted a few dishes she would later choose from.

The evening is filled with laughter, business, winks and never fading smiles. She shares with him that she is an Atlanta newbie and that she had only come because her job transferred.

He shares that he is an Atlanta native and, though very well-traveled, has never been a resident of any other state.

"The dessert is to die for, please tell me you saved room?" Josiah reaches across the table for Gabby's hand. "I would love to feed you the apple pie a la mode or the mint chocolate cheese cake."

He begins stroking the top of her hand while gazing into her eyes, waiting for her response and hoping for a yes.

Reclaiming her hand, sitting up straight, and clearing her throat Gabby gathers her words.

   "God has blessed me with two hands; I can manage feeding myself if you don't mind."

"Oh, but I do mind." Josiah doesn't back down.

The waiter arrives with the apple pie a la mode they had chosen. In that moment everything seems to start moving in slow motion for Gabby. Josiah picks up the dessert spoon and slices into the pie then scoops a bit of ice cream alongside it. As he moves the spoon towards her she feels her body going limp and her midsection tingles. Josiah's left hand resumes stroking hers as his right makes its way to her mouth. As she receives the sweet treat she couldn't help but let out a slight moan.

At first bite, Gabby was hooked, on more than just the pie. She had never been fed before and didn't want this to be the last time.

As she chews she tries to figure out whether the sensation that went through her was from the feeding or the stroking. By the time she swallowed she decides she doesn't care; it was a great feeling. One she hasn't felt in years.

While waiting on valet to bring the car around, they stood hand in hand recapping the evening. To her surprise and embarrassment, the release of her slight moan was on his list of funny events of the evening, right after the hostess tripping in the doorway when they arrived.

"Hey! Was it really that loud," Gabby asks dropping her face into her hand.

"I apologize, I got it all wrong. That moment actually falls under my list of sexiest moments from the evening." Josiah turns to Gabby pulling her into himself. "Along with your smile, your laughter and--"

"Are you sure you only had sweet tea," Gabby asks, interrupting his list. "It's chilly out tonight, where's the car?" She attempts to change the topic of conversation.

The car finally arrives. Josiah excuses the valet with a generous tip, insisting that he open and close his date's door. The smile that he was wearing quickly turns to a look of surprise. Just as Gabby climbs into the Mercedes she shares with him what she had almost forgotten herself.

CHAPTER 2

BLOCKING

AT THE CENTER OF IT ALL...A LOVE STORY

BLOCKING

The idea of becoming a nun was dancing through Gabby's mind when her phone buzzes.

Her mother's face invades her screen as the theme song to the show Family Matters came through the speaker.

Sorry mom, not right now, she thinks to herself while swiping the phone symbol left, ending the call.

Weeks have gone by and there has been no communication between Gabby and Josiah.

About a week or so in, Josiah called but didn't leave a message. Gabby dove deeper into work and Josiah deciding to travel visited friends up the East Coast.

===

"I am not sexually active and it has been that way for many years…and will remain that way until marriage." Is what poured from Gabby's mouth almost immediately after what she thought was a pretty amazing first date.

An awkward silence invaded the car while still sitting idle in front of the steakhouse. A knock on the window ended the silence; valet needed them to clear the way.

Josiah pulls away from the restaurant but drives slowly. He was trying to process what he had been told.

Although his intention was not to sleep with her that night, he found himself sexually attracted and looked forward to that time to come in the near future.

"The only reason I am telling you now and not later is because I didn't want you to get all turned on and then mad when you get turned down. I know I am gorgeous and I tend to be a bit of a flirt, soooo…" Gabby runs out of words during her attempt at an explanation.

Fifteen minutes into what seemed like a fifteen hour drive Josiah, who had been lost for words the entire time was finally able to speak.

"Look, I have never dated a woman who wasn't having sex. I mean, do you know anyone not doing it?"

Gabby bursts into laughter.

"The question is do I care who else is or isn't doing it. The answer is hell no." She told him vehemently.

Quickly she became frustrated and ended the conversation. Verbiage was not necessary to let him know as her body language spoke clearly to Josiah who agreed the conversation was over.

REINTRODUCTIONS

This wasn't the first time a man reacted shocked to Gabby's choice to abstain from sex. She never really cared what happened after she revealed her truth.

"Are you sure that was your momma and not Mr. Right?"

Gabby was joined by Verna and Tasha at their bi-weekly Sunday brunch spot in the city.

"No."

Gabby replies dryly, not looking up from her plate of cheese grits, eggs and fruit.

After an hour of what ifs and how to's, her girlfriends had convinced her she had no other choice but to call him back.

Gabby's work would consume all of her this week. Two networks airing major award shows within the month needed edit after edit. Also a local club had filmed for a well-known series and she had two hundred photos and signatures to go through to be sure to avoid any lawsuits.

By Friday night her bed was doing more than calling her. Finally making it home, it grabs and sucks her in so deep she didn't awake until late Saturday morning.

Cup of tea in hand, Gabby sits staring out her bay window watching cars and people come and go seemingly in a hurry.

Where could they be rushing to on a Saturday morning, she thinks to herself.

Glancing over at the Wonder Woman alarm clock gifted to her by her ex, Donald, who was convinced she was a wonder woman in her own right, she becomes anxious.

"I can still make it," she shouts as she jumps up from where she had been enjoying her R&R to race over to her closet and find the perfect outfit that says *"I'm cute enough to forgive."* A red short sleeved sweater, dark wash jeans, black knee high boots and leather jacket said just that.

A quick look in the mirror, and fluff to her naturally curly crowning glory, she runs out the door heading to an uncertain situation at a certain place of meeting.

She arrives at Center Coffee Shop, the grand clock in the courtyard down the way chimes loudly letting Gabby know it is noon. She was right on time.

As she walks in she begins skimming through the small shop slowly. It was quite busy as it usually is on Saturday afternoons.

Upon seeing no sign of Josiah, she decides he is late and stands in line to place an order.

"What would you like," the lady at the register asks. This took gabby by surprise; she had been watching the door so closely she didn't realize how fast the line was moving.

"You know, I am not sure today. What do you suggest?"

Before the young lady could finish her suggestions, Gabby's attention turns to the employee at the pick-up end of the counter shouting, "Caramel macchiato for Gabby!"

The lady calls the order out once more and, still, no one approaches to claim it.

"So you only claim things that don't have your name on it," a familiar voice asks Gabby from behind.

Controlling her excitement she turns slowly to meet the familiar voice face to face.

"Is that supposed to be for me?"

Josiah smiles as he walks past her to claim the coffee.

"Nah, but you better place your order quick, you holding up the line."

Now confused and a little embarrassed Gabby quickly places her order; hot cocoa with extra whipping.

She joins Josiah at a small table near the back of the shop.

"I knew you would eventually show up. I gave away my secret when we met. I figured, if you were paying attention, you would show up."

Gabby takes a sip of her hot cocoa. Proudly wearing her whip-stache she responds, "No, you didn't know. You were just hoping."

As the long overdue conversation went on, Josiah tells Gabby that he was not upset about her choice to wait until marriage and that he appreciates her being upfront about it.

"It never crossed my mind to not see you again," he confirmed. "You, unlike many women I have crossed paths with, dare to be different and do what is best for you. I admire that…it's kind of inspiring. I look forward to the challenge." He blushes.

"Many women huh?" Gabby jokes as they get up to leave.

PEEKING INTO THE PAST

Talking every day that week, they were very anxious and looking forward to being in the company of one another. Though it wasn't quite spring, it was a beautiful misty Saturday afternoon when they got together as previously agreed.

"Suwanee Park, beautiful place… are you familiar?"

Josiah was not familiar but he came prepared with a large plaid fleece blanket, grapes, cheese and a bottle of non-alcoholic wine to enjoy with Gabby in the park she described as beautiful.

In the middle of sharing childhood stories, Gabby notices a change in Josiah's demeanor.

His jaw line was tightening so she knew he was grinding his teeth.

"My mother…she was definitely something," he laughs through the pain in his eyes.

"What do you mean?" Gabby sits up and grabs his hand; she wanted him to know that she sensed his discomfort and was there for him.

"Nah, there is no need to ruin a beautiful day with ugly memories," Josiah says as he touches Gabby gently under her chin. "Don't ever lay down your virtue for anyone who is not willing to pick it up and hold it high for you."

In that moment Gabby felt as though she was awakened by Josiah's touch. The tone of his voice drummed with her heartbeat and their heavy breathing loudly in sync, creating an orchestra of the passion locked in between them both. Frozen at the eyes, they stare and become captured by the sound of their new found love.

Rain began to fall, running them and many other couples and families out of the park. Screams and laughter all around as people hurry to shelter.

A gentle kiss to Gabby's forehead ended their Saturday afternoon together. Having a meeting to get to, Josiah drops her off at home promising to reconnect later that evening.

"Church," Gabby shouts from her stoop, waving her hands to ensure she got his attention.

"What's wrong?" Josiah shouts back after noticing her hands in the air.

"Church! How about you pick me up in the morning and come to service with me? You don't have to dress fancy…it's a big church but has a very intimate and welcoming feel to it."

Gabby was smiling but her heart was about to beat right out of her chest. Many questions zipped through her mind after hearing what she had asked.

Am I pushing it? Am I asking too much too soon? Does he think I'm a holy-roller?

Interrupting her worrisome thoughts, Josiah replies, "I'll call you tonight and we'll talk about it."

As he drives off, Gabby stands confused. She was satisfied with his response because it wasn't a "no", but she couldn't help but wonder what was going through his mind.

To her surprise she would still be wondering when sleep finally came to her around midnight. He never called for her to ask.

CONTROL?

"Can I ride to brunch with you?" Tasha catches Gabby by surprise. She thought she hid herself well in the back row of the balcony section during service. She had no intention on attending brunch today.

"How did you get here?" Gabby asks confused.

"Joe. But I told him not to pick me up because I knew you'd be here. You haven't missed church since you joined. What's wrong with you?" Tasha stops in front of Gabby and stares with concerned eyes.

Gabby continues to walk on so Tasha runs alongside her and links arms as they walk.

"Nothing is wrong girl, just got some work to prep for two meetings tomorrow. Not to mention the pile of clothes on my closet floor to wash."

Unlinking arms and jumping back in front of Gabby, Tasha shouts, "So, you gonna skip Sunday brunch? The Sunday brunch you, me and Verna have been attending for the past 3 years? Remember, the only acceptable excuse is travel... you sure look 'in town' to me."

Gabby throws up her hands.

"You're right, I'm tripping."

Gabby mentally reminds herself that she is not to place any parts of her life on hold based on how she feels and that she has control over her emotions.

Monday morning Gabby is awakened to a "Good morning babe" text from Josiah. This is the first time she is hearing from him since his promise to call.

Accepting that she is still a bit in her emotions about it she decides not to respond. At least not until she feels she can speak out of a positive place. Besides, she needs her mind completely clear for all that was on her plate at work today.

After an unexpected four meetings later, at around seven that evening, Gabby was finally able to leave the office.

During the cab ride home she remembers the device that was neglected all day. Her phone had been in her pocketbook in the bottom drawer of her desk all day. She didn't have time to check it, even if she had the desire to.

"Unbelievable," she sighs while scrolling through her fourteen missed calls, with all but one being from Josiah.

"What have you been up to? Hard to get on the line these days," Gabby's but one caller complains. Wanting to be comfortable in the house when she spoke with Josiah, she called her mother back first.

"There is way too little truth in that sentence to have come out of your mouth young lady," Gabby playfully replies.

They talk during the entire twenty-seven minute long cab ride right on into the reheating and eating of leftover Sunday dinner from Tasha's house last night.

"I am so sorry that Gavin is behaving that way. I promise to call him and have a quick chat, as much as you don't want me to. Someone's got to! He's jeopardizing his scholarship and reputation. I'm his big sister, I'll handle it momma."

Patrice, Gabby's mother, knew how to get her assistance. She had a way of calling and playing helpless victim and Gabby would immediately do what she could so that her mother wouldn't have to deal with too much.

"Oh baby, you don't have to...I'm just so tired and he doesn't seem to listen to me. Your father--"

"That's enough," Gabby interrupts. "I said I would call him mom. I'm going to let you go for now, can't shower with phone in hand." Talks with her mother about her father were never too pleasant so Gabby had to end the call.

ALMOST DOESN'T COUNT

Showered, moisturized and relaxed, Gabby places a call to Josiah. To her surprise the call went straight to voicemail.

Suddenly there was a buzz from the intercom on the wall next to her front door. Without confirming the buzzer she anxiously pressed the open button hoping to soon hear a knock at her door. It was more like a pound at the door, but she got what she was hoping for.

Once open, Josiah storms in.

"How am I supposed to be a better man when my pops is still torn up about the woman that broke his heart so many years ago? If he doesn't let her go, it's going to kill him.

Church, she use to go to church...we all did. Sat in the front row all coordinated and

shi..."

He pauses and looks at Gabby apologetically.

"What are you talking about?" She asks confused while leading him to sit at the dining room table.

Gabby sits in one of the maple wood and brown leather chairs but Josiah places himself on his knees directly in front of her with his head in her lap.

Caressing the back of Josiah's freshly faded head, she decides to not say another word and just listen.

"Simplicity, honesty, and faithfulness...that's all I require. Can I trust you to be that?"

Not one tear in his eye but Gabby felt hers wailing up. She wasn't sure why the tears were coming or even if she should let them fall.

"I want to trust you, even love you Gabby…"

Josiah grabs Gabby firmly by her behind, pulling her closer to him. Suddenly she feels Josiah's lips softly kissing her legs. Then came the tears he had hidden so well as he grabs her tighter and kisses further up her thigh. Between the kisses and tears her thighs were almost as moist as her boy shorts were.

Fighting temptation was hard to do when feeling so weak. Her hand still placed on his head she finds herself pushing it into her as he kisses between her legs. Just as his hands find their way around her hips in an attempt to remove her leopard print boy shorts she feels her tears move quickly down her cheeks.

Grabbing his face with both hands and pulling him to hers she kisses away his tears.

"You can trust me…" Gabby promises to his crying eyes.

Gabby now standing, Josiah successfully removes her bottoms. His hands gently run up and down the back of her legs. Standing to face her, Josiah plants a hard and passionate kiss on her and Gabby instantly loses the little bit of control she thought she had left.

Josiah bends and wraps his arms firmly around her full hips and steadying his hands under her bottom he lifts her onto himself. When the parts that made him a man and her a woman make contact, Gabby is snapped back into her reality. She suddenly felt as though her spirit was shaking.

"We can't!" Gabby whispers jumping out of Josiah's arms, "We just can't"

Josiah was silent while watching Gabby redress herself with more clothes than he took off. With just a simple kiss to her forehead, Josiah walks himself out of her home.

Gabby stands in her lust and confusion for about ten minutes before taking another shower. As the lust washes off she finds herself praying to God for forgiveness followed by a request that Josiah get the answers he needs from God.

"Lord, heal his hurt and renew his strength...Amen"

BOUNDARIES

All month Gabby finds herself overworked and drained. Work and personal life had really done a number on her over the last few weeks. If she wasn't presenting to clients she was trying to get her family in order and keep friends happy. Not to mention maintain a healthy relationship with Josiah.

Since the night he came by to vent they decided they were not ready to uncover their pasts and wanted to work on their foundation first. He asked that Gabby never mention that night again and that he would talk about it when he was ready. Gabby was relieved that he felt this way. She had some skeletons in her closet that she was not quite ready to introduce him to but knew she would have to at some point.

In an attempt to avoid situations that would tempt their flesh sexually, they spent all their time out and about in the public eye and with friends. The boundaries set in place were necessary as their physical attraction to each other was undeniable.

After several months of dating with boundaries they decide they are strong enough to spend time alone in each other's homes.

A month in they attempted a movie night at Josiah's townhouse but every onscreen touch or kiss aroused their flesh. Halfway through the movie Josiah asked Gabby to leave. Luckily they both found humor in the dismissal.

While setting the dining room table for their long awaited candle lit dinner that evening there was a knock at Gabby's door.

She looks at her wristwatch and raised her eyebrow; Josiah was not due to arrive for another couple of hours.

Looking through the peep-hole Gabby gasps and slowly steps away from the door.

"I know you're home"

Her past was speaking to her from the other side of her door.

Not responding, Gabby stands there trying to make sense of why her past was at her door after all these years.

"Come on Gab, open up."

Reluctantly Gabby twists the lock and slowly opens the door to her past.

CHAPTER 3

TRUTH BE TOLD

TRUTH BE TOLD

Racing to beat the early morning traffic, Josiah throws on his jacket and runs out the door for an important meeting. Chad Linden, also a financial advisor out of the west coast, had expressed an interest in working with Josiah last year at a leadership conference in Reno. Though they exchanged business cards they had not connected until a week ago when Josiah received a straight forward email:

"I'll be in town, let's connect, Monday at eight we'll do breakfast and business."

Josiah, always prompt and prepared, believed that right on-time was late. So you can understand the disappointment and frustration he has when he arrives to the restaurant at 7:58am.

To his surprise, Chad had yet to arrive. This didn't excuse his being late but it calmed his concern with how Chad was going to react to it, as he feels any business minded person believes as he does regarding preparation and promptness. Josiah's prompt and prepared mentality not only moved him forward in his career but was also one of the determining factors for anyone who was looking to move forward with him. At this point Chad has shown himself unreliable, Josiah quickly becomes uninterested.

The sun was high and the wind was still. Josiah, taking a walk through the city, enjoys the calmness of his surroundings. The calmness turns to chaos with just one phone call.

Claude, his business partner was in an uproar about the meeting Josiah walked out on this morning.

"Technically, I didn't walk out on anyone…there was no one there to walk out on." Josiah defends himself.

"Chad arrived right after you left. You have to learn patience or we're never going to grow to the level of--"

"No" Josiah interrupts. "We wouldn't be where we are today if we just dealt with anyone and allowed them to disrespect what we worked hard to build. JC Financial is not going to bow down to anyone just because their thinking about investing. I demand respect before doing business."

A now furious Josiah decides to make his way to the gym and blow off some steam. He needs to calm himself for tonight. Gabby was preparing a candle lit dinner at her condo and he wants to be in a good place mentally for their first night alone in a while.

MEMORY LANE

By five that evening, Josiah was in the car and headed northwest to enjoy the night with Gabby. He is not scheduled to arrive until seven but there were a couple stops he needed to make on the way.

"Hello Miss Francis" Josiah calls out.

"Oh Jo-Jo, I haven't seen you in months. Who is she?" Miss Francis inquires walking over to squeeze Josiah.

Laughing, Josiah plants a kiss on her cheek.

"I need a bouquet of your best for the best." He answers.

While waiting for Miss Francis to work her magic he walks around the flower shop reading the different thank you cards hanging all around that she has received over the years. She has mended marriages, kicked off relationships and buried many people with her beautiful flowers. She drove hours every day from her farm, with miles of land where she grows her business as well as her meals, into the city to run her shop.

Miss Francis provided the flowers for his parent's wedding, he remembers. Chrysanthemums, his mother's favorite, were along the aisles of the church and in the center of each table at the reception. Josiah could remember it like it was yesterday; he was six years old and his mother was the most beautiful woman in the world.

"You'll get a beauty just like your mother," Miss Francis gleamed at Josiah as she strategically placed each flower in their place.

By the time Josiah was sixteen, he couldn't stand the sight of his mother.

"Did you marry her heart or her beauty," He remembers asking his father on his eighteenth birthday when he brought home his date for the prom and his father didn't approve of her looks. He never responded but that was fine with Josiah because he already knew the answer.

"How's this," Miss Francis asks, interrupting his walk down memory lane.

In her hands she held a beautiful assortment of flowers bound by a mauve ribbon. Josiah smiles, pleased.

A major accident was causing major traffic on the interstate so Josiah places a call to Gabby to let her know he was en route but, to his surprise, there was no answer… not even by the fourth try. Now even more anxious to arrive, to settle his thoughts, he pressed three on the radio which plays instrumental R&B until he arrives at his destination.

About five minutes away from Gabby's place his instrumental tunes were replaced with the standard Bluetooth ringtone through his speakers.

Call from Winston, the screen informs him.

Winston has been in Josiah's life since elementary school. He was eight and Josiah was seven when they met. They didn't find out they shared a bloodline until high school when Josiah's mother was the host of Winston's graduation party.

"Hey Bro, how you been?"

Josiah never really got into the "bro" thing but Winston was more like a best friend which made "bro" acceptable. He had other siblings, a younger brother and two younger sisters, which his mother birthed but was not as welcoming to terms of endearment from them.

"I been alright man, what's going on with you?" Josiah replies.

An excited Winston shares with his brother that he has popped the big question to his girlfriend of three years and she said yes. The theme was winter wonderland and the colors were mint green, gold and tan.

"I would love to have you standing right next to me at the altar Bro. Would you do me the honor of being my best man?"

SKELETONS

Josiah, though very excited for his brother had some reservations about the offer. He knew that Winston marrying Arin was good and that Arin was a good woman from what he could tell. But he couldn't believe his older brother reached a point of trusting enough to marry, even after watching their mother parade around stepping on hearts.

"Wow, that's big! Congratulations and please give Arin my love. I want to be there for you man. Let me take a look into my schedule for the next couple months and get back with you on it. I know the role of Best Man requires some time and attendance. I just want to make sure I can be all in for you. You understand?"

Winston, laughing off his doubt agrees to a callback on his response. Winston was fully aware of Josiah's feelings and fears about trust, love and marriage. After a few more minutes of small talk the brothers said goodbye.

Josiah parks and is now even more anxious to head upstairs and talk to Gabby about Winston's engagement and how he's feeling about it all.

As he walks toward the building, he wonders if he should even mention it to her. He didn't want to open up that painful chapter of his past, but knows Gabby would ask why he's so uptight about his best friend's wedding.

He would also have to tell her that Winston was more than just his best friend. She knows Josiah to be an only child.

She deserves to know that truth... besides this is a sure fire way to guarantee no sex. Digging into my past is far from sexy

Josiah finds himself laughing out loud. He can't wait to see Gabby's face and laugh with her.

"I'll be right down," Gabby speaks quickly through the intercom after Josiah buzzes.

He stands there confused because he is usually buzzed up.

A teary eyed Gabby appears and just stands on the other side of the glass door silently mouthing the words *'I'm sorry'* between every loud sob.

Now, not only confused but also concerned, Josiah begins pulling on the door pleading with Gabby to let him in. He wants to comfort her even though he doesn't know what was causing her discomfort.

A tenant of the building was coming in behind Josiah, relieved that he steps away so she could unlock the door. Before she could, Gabby opens and holds it for her.

Gabby was still holding the door open but Josiah didn't follow the tenant in.

"If you want me to go, I will but I would much rather stay and talk about whatever has you acting like this," Josiah informs her.

Unable to say anything, Gabby cries harder.

"You know what? We don't have to talk about it. Whatever you want," he pleads.

DANIEL

The elevator opens and out walks Gabby's past. Tall, well built and dressed in a crisp designer suit with matching designer shoes. He approaches her and Josiah feels anger building up inside his chest. The kiss to Gabby's forehead causes the built-up anger to release itself.

"What the hell is this Gabby?" Josiah throws the flowers to the ground and stands firm and confident not taking his eyes off of hers.

"Hey, I'm Daniel," Gabby's past shifts the small brown paper bag he's holding into his left hand, extending his right toward Josiah for a shake. Josiah, still looking Gabby in the eye, never extends his hand. Gabby steps between them and gently lowers Donald's.

"No need to fake friendly. Just go," she pushes him along.

Josiah steps away from the doorway to let him pass. As he is exiting, he stops and looks Josiah square in the eye.

"She's Wonder Woman, you know? She's really something," Daniel says, reaching into the bag he's been holding. "That's why I got her this," he smirks, holding up the Wonder Woman alarm clock he had given her on their one year anniversary.

Gabby had cherished this gift, not because of who gave it to her but what it meant. Someone thought she was SUPER. This gift came at a time when she was struggling with accepting that for herself. She no longer had a need for it. She now knows who she is in Christ and in life. She kindly thanked him for the boost of confidence many years ago but acknowledges that it was time to let go of those types of memories.

"Funny how that works, right man? We don't know what we got til it's gone." Josiah, shifting his eyes from Daniel, grabs Gabby's hand letting the door close, leaving Daniel to stare from the outside.

This was his place, an onlooker. He no longer holds a place in Gabby's heart no matter the history between them which he spent the last two hours bringing up in hopes that it would rekindle feelings for him.

"We have a child together Gabby, why can't we work it out as a family?"

Daniel's attempt to bring light to their past love brought darkness to Gabby's future. With every word she could only think of how Josiah would react if he knew about her child.

"Did he hurt you?" Josiah grabs Gabby by the face, snatching her thoughts away.

"Gabby, what happened?" He continues, looking for truth in her eyes but Gabby is paralyzed. Her thoughts are fixed on the outcome of telling Josiah what she has done.

He realizes no words are going to come from her. He leads her upstairs where they would spend the evening laying together watching late night reruns of what use to be day time TV. Both had something to tell, but both knew this wasn't the right time. Body heat, soft kisses and laughs was all they needed from each other tonight, and that's all they would give.

HOME AGAIN

The week zips by for Josiah. Barely getting time to spend with Gabby over the past week, he thinks of the last night they spent together and smiles.

After a Saturday afternoon meeting, Josiah took to the highway en route to Fayetteville to visit his father for a few days. He likes that it only takes about an hour to drive to his father's place. The drive gives him time to prepare for any foolishness that might occur.

Being an only child to his father, Josiah takes great pride in caring for him in his old age. He makes it a point to visit at least once a week, almost always spending the night.

"JJ, my boy," Robert, Josiah's uncle, says as he greets him at the door. "Hey, didn't know you were going to be here! I would have brought my scrabble board and gave you a good beatin' had I known." They laugh while embracing each other.

"Your father is resting now, he and I been camping. We ended up running through them woods from some deer. Can you believe that? They must'a known we had hunted their kinfolk last huntin' season." Uncle Robert laughs with a raspy laugh.

He had been tobacco free for the past two years but smoked like a chimney for thirty-eight years before that. Robert gave Josiah his first puff when he was twelve. Josiah hated it and never tried smoking anything again. He was very close with his Uncle Robert. He and his wife, Shelly, would comfort Josiah, as he grew up, when his mother and father would fight.

"Your father is a man that loves with all his heart. You be that man too. No matter what it looks like for your father, the woman God has for you will appreciate that love."

If it hadn't been for Uncle Robert and Aunt Shelly's solid relationship, he would have doubted true love. Aunt Shelly passed of lung cancer three years ago, this prompted Uncle Robert to stop smoking. He blames himself for her death because she never lifted a cigarette to her mouth her entire life.

Josiah prepares dinner for the men: candied yams, collard greens, fried chicken, corn bread and macaroni and cheese. He enjoys cooking mainly because this was something he learned from his mother. She would have him in the kitchen with her every Sunday preparing dinner after church service.

She never stayed to enjoy dinner with him and his father though. She always had to leave by five on Sunday evenings, not returning until Wednesday morning, just in time to see him off to school.

Not once did he question her absence…didn't even take the time to wonder why. He was just glad that she always came back.

"You know your brother is getting married? Your mother is in over her head planning it all," his father says between bites.

"Ooh wee, this some good cookin', boy! Why we ain't planning your wedding? You know, a man can just as easily win the heart of a woman by cooking just like a woman does a man's. You tried it," Uncle Robert asks, changing the subject after seeing the look in Josiah's eyes. He is certain that his nephew is not in the mood to speak about his mother's other children and what she is doing in their lives.

"You know, I haven't tried Uncle Robert, but I think I will give it a shot." Laughter joins them at the table.

The night was full of powdered donuts, popcorn and old western movies. None of these were on Josiah's top 10 list of great things but he did enjoy the company of his father, and his uncle being there was a bonus.

"When we get to come to your end and see your nice fancy place in the city? Or is it that you don't have space in your city world for country folk?" Uncle Robert lets out another raspy laugh.

"Always welcome sir, I mean that."

Morning now here, Josiah lays out pastries and brews a fresh pot of coffee for the men to enjoy together before he gets on the road. He enjoys these early mornings out on his father's porch. The three bedroom, four bath one level home sat on a corner lot wrapped by a great bed of flowers which were planted and maintained by none other than Miss Francis whom lives about twenty minutes away from his father. The dining room had a sliding door that lead out to the porch which he furnished with classy and comfortable patio furniture.

Josiah sits with a cup of coffee and looks out over the yard where he imagined his children running around and playing. He closes his eyes and sees his beautiful, faithful wife sitting right next to him also with coffee in hand.

His and Her coffee mugs would be nice, he smiles, thinking to himself.

Opening his eyes he looks over at the empty seat next to him and then at his watch. He decides to call Gabby.

"How's country living?" Gabby asks, jokingly.

Josiah was in no joking mood, "I miss you."

He says with a hint of desperation in his voice. Picking up on it, Gabby instantly connects and feels the desperation bubbling up inside.

"I miss you too babe. When--"

Josiah interrupts Gabby's attempt to talk through the feelings trapped in the phone line.

"We have to get this right. You trust me? Because I trust you. I think we can win at anything we find ourselves competing for. You know?"

Heavy breathing fills the line.

"Love is not simple. If it were, people would be more welcoming of it…instead most of us fear it. It's not just me."

"You fear love?" Gabby asks surprised.

"Where we go depends on where we start…no lies, no surprises." Josiah continues, ignoring Gabby's question.

Where did we start? Gabby wondered.

THE BOX

Pastries half eaten and pot of coffee empty, Josiah prepares to leave his father's home.

"Boy, you got that duffel bag over your shoulder like you headin' out to the army!" Robert salutes Josiah.

"Now go'on, be safe and call when you make it." He pats Josiah on the back and heads for the sofa to sit and watch his favorite court show.

Leaning in for a hug, his father whispers, "You don't have to fear that which has no control over you. You can choose where it starts and where it ends up."

A variety of hip-hop artists got Josiah from Fayetteville to Atlanta. He bobbed his head the entire way home with his mind completely free and clear.

As he pulls into the driveway he notices the screen door is propped open by a medium size box. Josiah walks into his home dropping his overnight bag at the bottom of the stairs as he makes his way to the dining room table where he places the box marked 'fragile'.

He studies the hand-written label which listed his entire name, Josiah Justin Emmit, but he couldn't connect the penmanship with anyone in particular. He walks into the kitchen to grab a pair of scissors when he notices the red light flashing on his voicemail system. There was rarely a call on the land line, let alone a message. He smiles thinking about how Gabby laughed hysterically when she discovered he had it.

"Take my hand and walk into the new age…don't worry, it's not too scary," she joked.

Josiah walks back over to the box, scissors in hand but not before pressing play on the answering machine.

"Look, there's so much I need to say…frankly I just don't want to. I just want you to know…well, I know that you know because I've told you before but I want you to believe. Believe that I love you…I always have. You are special to me and I would love to get to know the man that you've become."

Staring at the label on the box while the message was playing, he was finally able to identify the handwriting.

Josiah finds himself angry. Pushing the box across the table he decides opening it was pointless, at least now.

"Hey, I am back in the city. Can you come by?"

Marvin Gaye was filling the house with Love and Happiness while Josiah washed the road off himself.

"make you come home early, yeah…" Gabby enters the bathroom singing along to the record.

"Join me?" Josiah pulls the curtain back, inviting Gabby in.

She pauses and stares as the water hits hard against his milk chocolate skin. Being in business for himself, he was often stressed; Gabby knew this led him to the gym to blow off steam. But she was caught off guard by the result of his frequent trips there.

"Stress much?" Gabby jokes as she struggles to keep her eyes above his waist.

Josiah steps out the shower quickly grabbing Gabby by the hand and into the shower with him. Gabby is fully dressed but never felt so exposed in her life. As the water runs over her white t-shirt and blue jeans she throws her head back into the water as Josiah kisses her neck slowly and embraces her wet clothed body tightly.

Feeling off balance, Gabby places her hands on the glass shower wall while Josiah's hands travel underneath her wet t-shirt rubbing her back, while his lips never leave her neck.

Marvin's "Love and Happiness" turns into Maxwell's "Sumthin Sumthin" mellow version making this entire situation harder to fight.

"Come on babe, let's go play scrabble." Just as he led her into the shower, Josiah respectfully leads her out.

"Wow, you look amazing."

Gabby gives Josiah the side-eye as she throws her clothes into the dryer.

"Yeah, this football jersey is really tailored to my body…perfect fit," she teases back.

Second round of scrabble and second victory for Josiah, Gabby feels it is time to spill her beans.

She places a hand on Josiah's and stares waiting for his eyes to come up and connect to hers. But they never did, not in that moment.

Josiah grabs the remote and turns on the stereo to let Kem swoon them through the speakers. He takes Gabby by the hand and asks, "May I have this dance?"

SHE

Gabby, only 5'2" tall, rests her head on Josiah's stomach. She loves how he towers over her, making her feel protected. He holds her tighter and the smooth tunes continue to rock their bodies slowly.

"I have so much I want to tell you. How can I when every moment is this sweet," he asks, finding Gabby's eyes.

"Wouldn't be lemonade without a sour lemon, no matter how much sugar is added," she assures him.

Their eyes agreed that they can no longer let another day pass without getting their secrets off their chest.

"I want nothing more than to make this work with you. Please tell me that no matter what is said, we can continue to move forward with what we're trying to build?"

"Yes!" Gabby shouts relieved that he feels this way.

Grabbing at her sterling silver butterfly necklace she looks down at the floor in deep thought.

Could his news be worse than mine?

The ringing of Josiah's landline broke her thoughts.

"You going to get that?" after the fourth ring Gabby was wondering at what point the voice messaging system would pick up.

It wouldn't. After the message Josiah received earlier he decided to disconnect the voicemail system.

"She's going to keep calling, and every time she calls she is probably going to leave a voicemail so...I should have went unlisted."

Confused Gabby sits straight up at the edge of the charcoal gray chase where they sat to share.

"She?"

Josiah calmly gets up and walks into the kitchen where, like the voice message machine cord, he snatches the phone cord out of the wall.

"Yeah, 'she' Gabby. She has ruined my life. She has messed me all up in the head."

Silence falls; Josiah not knowing where to start and Gabby unsure of what questions she should ask of the million that were now flooding her mind...

"Look" they speak up in unison.

Night has stolen the little bit of sunlight from the windows of Josiah's home and just as the shadows begin to form on the walls, the walls of Josiah's heart begin to go dark. The fear of Gabby walking out after hearing what he has to say kept him silent.

"Does she love me as much as she claims?" Josiah thought out loud.

Tears now falling from Gabby's eyes she knew that it was just as she thought.

"So what, you're torn," she asks trying to remain calm.

"Yeah, I am torn…I want to tell you everything but I don't want to tell you too much because you will lose understanding of me."

Disgusted Gabby jumps up from the chase and moves quickly to the dryer to retrieve her clothes which she hopes are dry after only spinning for twenty minutes.

"I was going to break my promise to myself…to God!" she screams.

"I should have known that this was all too good to be true. Let me tell you something you probably haven't gathered about me in this little time of, of…whatever it is we've been doing; I come second to no one. I am confident in who I am therefore I know what I deserve and it's not a torn man!"

Josiah falls to his knees and joins Gabby in the crying game. He reaches out to her, pleading for her to calm down.

"I don't know why I couldn't just tell you my issue. At least I am not on the damn fence about anything. I made a decision and I stuck with it. Why regret it? It's my past. You're probably not even man enough to accept the fact that I have a--"

"Gabby, stop!" Josiah quickly interrupts. "This is what I can't do. Either we are going to sit and talk about this like adults or not talk at all. You think you know but baby, you really don't. Sit here and let me talk to you, calmly."

"Calmly?" Gabby jumps back. "You got up and snatched the cord out the wall."

THE LETTER

Minutes of back and forth took place before finally calming themselves. They sit and brainstorm on ways to tell their issues without a big blowup. They decide to write them down.

Josiah sitting at the dining room table wrote out his secrets. Gabby upstairs sprawled across his neatly made king size bed did the same.

A tender kiss to the forehead and they exchanged letters which were sealed in envelopes.

"I'll text you when I get home so that we can open them at the same time," she reminds him.

Envelopes in hand, they separate for the night.

Josiah can't part with the letter, even to use the bathroom. Only fifteen minutes of Gabby's absence and already he's started checking his phone every two minutes anxious for the go.

Exactly thirty minutes later Josiah's phone rings and Gabby's face fills his screen.

"Don't open it. I am so sorry that I didn't wait until I got home. The cab ride seemed so long and…just please, don't open it."

Without responding Josiah tears open the envelope. Gabby, now on speaker phone is pleading for him to stop. He doesn't, she only knows this because the line disconnects.

"She's my mother! Why is every woman I meet my mother? How do you just give a child away? We'd be better off never born," he questions Gabby's truth in the mirror.

Several attempts to get Josiah back on the line failed. Gabby climbs in bed holding Josiah's letter; reading it over and over and crying until finally she drifts to sleep.

Gabby,

I love you more than you'll probably ever know or understand. I have never met a woman that made me believe in love so deep. You are the perfect summer day, you know that breeze that hits you when the sun is completely unbearable Nothing like my mother. She, is the cold that chokes you in the night of winter. As beautiful as she was she was as ugly as a troll inside. She ran around having children by men other than my father, while he and I sat at home wondering if or when she would return. For as long as I can remember I would sit and wonder does she even love me? I didn't have to wonder that about you. I couldn't imagine you having a child and just leaving it to live your life. Granted, she came around but she wasn't present. Her life meant more than my future. I have been shut-in and held back because of her and how she left me needing and wanting her. You came along and opened the door setting me free. It's not going to be easy, because of the relationship with my mother I am messed up. Winston… well, he's more than just my best boy; he's my brother. Sorry I lied to you but I am embarrassed by my mother's choices in life. It will take some time and work but I couldn't imagine a better person being at my side while I grow to love deeper and stronger…I want to trust you.

CHAPTER 4

UNTIL NEXT TIME

UNTIL NEXT TIME

"Don't forget your toiletry bag."

Verna appears from the bathroom with more than just Gabby's toiletry bag.

"I'm going on a business trip, not dying. Put my pearls back where you got them…and my diamond earrings too," she instructs her friend in a kind but stern tone.

As Gabby sorts through her clothes to decide on what's needed for her six day trip to Los Angeles, she also takes a moment to sort through her feelings about not having spoken to Josiah for six days.

Several attempts have been made to reach him on his mobile as well as his office phone. The one-way calling game had become draining to Gabby causing her to give up by day three.

"I know you think I am giving up too easy. Truth is he brought this on himself. Why should I walk around with guilt about something I've already been forgiven for? If he can't forgive then it's his issue not mine," Gabby spats emotionally to her suitcase as she refuses to make eye contact with Verna whose stare is burning the side of Gabby's face.

"I couldn't care less about whatever it is you and Josiah got going on…you're on your way to Los Angeles! Leave that mess here girl."

The ladies laugh out loud in unison falling onto the floor. Gabby was laughing but crying on the inside.

Could this really be it? One mistake from years ago will keep me from a future with someone I feel is right for me? Gabby wonders.

The alarm buzzes bright and early at five. Alerting Gabby that it is time to pull herself together to head to the airport. Rolling to her left she rolls into Verna.

"The things we do for love," Verna mumbles, pushing Gabby off of her.

Verna stayed over to drive Gabby to the airport this morning. It took a lot of convincing, though, as she had plans with a guy she has been pursuing for some time whom just so happened to be wide open when her friend needed her.

"Did you hear that?"

Verna and Gabby's attention is immediately directed toward the door just as the second knock comes.

"Who's there?" Gabby calls out as she slowly makes her way to look through the peep hole.

"Can we talk?"

To Gabby's surprise, hearing his voice irritated her. Still silent on her side of the door, Josiah goes on.

"Look, You don't know enough about my past to understand why I reacted the way I did. I mean you got an idea from my letter but I just really need to share everything with you. Look Gabby, trusting a woman has not been easy, hell it hasn't been possible...not until you came along and stole my cup of coffee. Do you know I had to re-order my cup that day?"

Gabby could feel the warmth of Josiah's smile on the door. She was resting her head and hands on it listening closely with a smiling heart.

"I love you Gabby, more important than that...I trust you. I didn't give you a chance to explain your letter and I would love for you to, if you even still care to talk to me."

The tears run down as Gabby ponders on her response. Verna comes behind Gabby offering affection.

Gabby turns to her friend and wipes her tears.

"I have a flight to catch," Gabby says aloud as she walks away from the door back to the bathroom to splash water on her face.

Twenty minutes pass, suitcase zipped, shoes on and keys in hand.

"Watch out LA, Gabby's on her way!" Verna smiles and grabs her friend by the arm.

Opening the door Gabby's heart drops a bit. To her surprise, Josiah didn't wait. Also to her surprise, she didn't care as much as she had braced herself to.

LA

After only two days in Los Angeles Gabby has forgotten all about her fall out with Josiah. Somehow Josiah knew she was carefree, looking at her phone she notices eight missed calls, all from him.

"Look, I know…I know. Let's just talk," was all Josiah could get out over four voice messages.

Gabby carelessly places her cell phone back in her beach bag and runs to join her co-workers in the ocean.

"That is a really nice color on you," Nathan, Gabby's co-worker, compliments.

"Honestly, I hate green but I really like the style of this bathing suit."

Nathan laughs hysterically.

Gabby's smile fades and an eyebrow rises.

"Didn't know I was a comedian; let alone putting on a show at the moment…where do I collect my check?"

Nathan gently places his hands on Gabby's wet shoulders.

"You are the only person I know that says *bathing suit*!" Nathan could barely get out his words without going back to laughing hysterically.

A smile creeps upon Gabby's face letting Nathan know that she agrees, at least a little bit, that her choice of words are out dated. Two hours full of splashing and sun bathing, Gabby has had her share of the beach.

"Gabby…wait up" Nathan shouts, running up the beach to catch Gabby as she heads to her room.

"How about dinner tonight? You don't have to wear green… I'd like to see what color you think looks good on you and I'll let you know if I agree," he jokes.

"Oh, so you're the comedian of the hour," Gabby jokes back. "Who's all coming and where?" Gabby tugs at her hair forcing her thick tresses' into a fluffy, wet ponytail as she waits for Nathan's response.

Nathan looks away bashfully, kicking up the sand beneath his feet.

At that moment Gabby understood the invitation was just for her. Grabbing Nathan's face with her hands she smiles in his eyes and kindly accepts.

FORGIVENESS

After an hour of pacing back and forth Josiah finally stands still, looking down at the floor where he had been pacing expecting to see tracks of his moving thoughts.

"How did you do it? How did you get past the trust issues and let your guard down to fully love…trust?" Josiah cries out to his older brother.

He had placed the call to Winston in the midst of his pacing but didn't know what to say. Winston, not familiar with this side of Josiah, kindly waits on the opposite end of the line before speaking as Josiah grunts and breathes heavily into the phone.

"You have to understand, mom's issue was hers…not ours or the women we chose to have in our lives. You have to reach a point where you care enough about yourself to forgive mom and move on with your life."

Tears well up in the corners of Josiah's eyes and he begins breathing even heavier. Throwing his head back in an attempt to keep the tears in, he lets out a shout.

"Forgiveness?"

It wasn't until this very moment that Josiah even acknowledged the fact that he hasn't forgiven his mother. He knew he had an issue with her presence, or lack thereof, during his childhood but forgiveness was not the issue, or so he thought.

"Did you tell her that you forgive her? How?"

Josiah, now seeking instruction from his brother, assuming there was a specific process to reach the point he was at and that he had completed it already.

"Not at all," Winston admits. "I told myself and God. I needed to forgive her to heal me, not the other way around."

Josiah, despite the tears that were struggling to remain in the corners of his eyes bursts in to laughter, pushing the tears out. Only now they aren't tears of pain but tears of joy. Confused but glad to hear the laughter, Winston joins in.

"I forgive her man… I have to because if I forgive her I can forgive Gabby. I don't even care about all the baby stuff anymore."

"Baby stuff?" Winston, still chuckling yet still confused asks.

Josiah hadn't disclosed much detail about what he is dealing with in regards to his and Gabby's current relationship situation. At this point, Winston was just trying to piece whatever Josiah told him together to try and make sense out of it all.

Winston accepted his brother's attempts to be private and never judged or tried to pry. He took what he could get because he valued their relationship.

The next evening Josiah found himself posted outside of Gabby's building. He had only been sitting there for about ten minutes before a cab pulls up and Gabby jumps out. He watches as the driver pulls her luggage from the trunk. He smiles at the sight of her.

"Gabby…" Josiah shouts to her, waving his hand as he dashes across the street.

Now face to face with Gabby, Josiah gives what he believes is a tranquilizing stare in hopes that she would fall victim to it.

"Babe, let's not do this anymore. Let's stop all the foolishness and make this right…now," He reaches for Gabby's hand as he pleads to make amends.

"We are in the middle of the street, it's drizzling rain and I am tired. Let's set a time to meet sometime this week. I have a lot to put together for my upcoming presentation…and what are you doing here anyway? How did you know I was coming home tonight?" Gabby snaps, tucking her hands into her pockets. This let Josiah know she is immune to his tranquilizing eyes.

"Gabby, I--"

"Come on Josiah, I know you love me. I love you, too. It's just that now is not the time to talk about everything," she says, staring seriously at Josiah. "When you miss a train at the station you can't demand one show up right that second to take you where you need to go… you have to check the schedule and wait."

Shaking his head, Josiah turns to head back to his car but just before he made the dash once again, he looks at Gabby one last time.

"Damn girl, can you stop with the independent, I am the last woman on earth attitude? I wasn't going to say I love you…I know you already are aware of that." As he turns to go, Josiah takes out and throws a piece of paper he had been holding onto the ground which landed at Gabby's feet.

"It's not an attitude, it's just me…I am independent and I am the first and last one of me on this earth," Gabby yells to Josiah as he climbs into his car and drives off.

She picks up the piece of paper and tucks it into the pocket of her pea coat and heads upstairs.

A shower, a few chapters of Psalms and two warm cups of ginger tea later, Gabby realizes her wrong. But after reflecting over her and Josiah's relationship, she realizes some of the walls she let down because he made her feel comfortable. At the same time, she realizes while she was dropping walls he was putting them up. This put her back in square one...in which she had done no wrong.

She goes into her front closet and removes the piece of paper from the pocket.

> *"I have given birth to a child but I am not a mother. I was very young and had so many plans for my future so I gave the child up for adoption. All that I know is the child was born May 6th healthy and weighed eight pounds even. I chose to not know the sex or the information of the family that was chosen to raise the child. Daniel, the guy who was at my place that evening, he is who fathered the child. I do not regret my decision and do not care for opinion on my choice...just thought you should know."*

She falls asleep while holding the letter to her chest.

HEALING PLACE

Gabby, still trying to get off LA time drags herself into work every day. By Thursday, coworkers were concerned.

"Hey mamma, why are you so gloomy? Your presentation is in a few hours...you got this or what?"

Saundra, the newbie, still hadn't caught on to the fact that she was not interested in conversing with her. Although Gabby considered her to be a nice girl, she also considered her to be annoying.

"I'll be fine," Gabby responds.

As usual, Gabby was able to perk up for her presentation and nail it. Performing her duties in a professional manner has never been an issue, regardless of what she may be dealing with.

"I see a lot of myself in you…you should be running your own business," Josiah once told her.

That evening, to celebrate, Gabby went out and bought half of a tiramisu cake to eat while catching up on her favorite shows recorded on her DVR.

"*Nathan?*" Verna shouts through the phone.

She had called and interrupted Gabby's night so she used this time to tell her about the candle lit dinner with her co-worker that never happened.

"Girl, calm down. I gave him your number so be expecting a call. I told him that you would love to get to know him.

Verna breaks out into laughter, "I want to get to know his mini-me first…that will determine whether getting to know him is worth it or not."

"Figures," Gabby says. "I am sure his mind is on that same path, that's why I gave him your number. Thank me later," she laughs.

Saturday afternoon Gabby finds herself seated at a small table in the back corner of Center Coffee shop. She came prepared with a speech; she had even practiced calming exercises for when he says things to boil her water. Unfortunately she hadn't prepared calming exercises for when he says no words. Josiah was a no show.

Gabby has decided to face him and deal with the issues. She is beginning to feel terrible about the couple times she has brushed him off. When Nathan asked her to dinner during her work trip it reminded her that she no longer wanted to be in the world of dating. She had something real with Josiah and as long as they were both willing they could make it through.

Her emotions now taking over after two hours of sitting there, she jumps up and storms out.

Placing two calls to Josiah's cell, Gabby is now beyond angry because both went straight to voicemail. She stands in front of the shop staring at the logo confused. All this time she has believed the coffee shop was their healing place.

Knots form in her throat as she fights to keep herself from crying. In the middle of the battle with her tears, her phone vibrates in her hand. The battle was won by her tears as she answers.

"Now is not a good time!" Gabby got straight to the point and without a response, she hangs up.

After several hours of walking through the park, the rain begins to fall over Gabby's broken heart as well as her hard head.

Showered and cozy in her favorite nook of her sectional, she scrolls through her phone: twelve text messages, four missed calls and two voicemail messages. Gabby runs her fingers through her dripping wet curls and takes a deep breath before hitting the call button.

"What exactly is it that you are chasing, Gabby?" Her mother's voice, though quiet and calm, deafened Gabby for a moment. She and her mother formed a special connection over the last few years which started shortly after her father's passing. Whenever she really needed direction, her mother would call. Even when Gabby was at home, her mother would show up. Gabby once joked with her mother and questioned, "Did daddy's spirit to love on me just jump into you once he died?"

Gabby's thoughts took over the conversation, unknown to her mother who continues on.

"God continues to make a way for you to do and have all your heart desires because you seek Him first. His word says in Matthew 6, somewhere in there, 'seek first the kingdom of God and all his righteousness and he'll surprise you with all that other stuff you want.'"

Gabby heard none of the truth her mother was sharing. Her mind was occupied by the initial question…*what are you chasing, Gabby?*

Suddenly Gabby felt the Holy Spirit rest over her and her hearing returns.

"God has already forgiven you but you must forgive yourself to move forward. Maybe you need to speak to someone once a week or something to talk about how you're really dealing with the things of your past."

Gabby sits up, eyes wide open. A light bulb goes on in her head. She quickly thanks her mother for the few words that she did hear and kindly let her know she had to let her go for now. Glad that she appeared to have made an impact with her words, she happily hung up.

THE CAR

The heavy wind was pushing Gabby around as she made her way to Josiah's house. She hopped out of the cab a block away so that he wouldn't see her coming. She wants to surprise him just as he did her the morning she was headed to the airport. Hoping he would welcome her despite her reaction, she approaches the door.

Three knocks and a couple rings of the doorbell, no answer. He was surely home because his Mercedes as well as a Toyota Camry was parked in the driveway. The blinds were shut all around the house so there was no way for Gabby to see in. Looking at her cell phone, she considers calling but at this point is afraid of no response or even the wrong response if he were to answer.

Gabby walks over to the Camry for a peek inside. The windows are tinted but up close she is able to see what's inside; loose coins scattered over the floor of the passenger side and a silver coffee mug occupied the back coffee holder between the bucket leather seats. On the seat sat a brown briefcase and a pair of blue and black walking shoes.

Continuing her snooping into the backseat she discovers a pink and white duffel bag with a black pair of yoga pants partially hanging out. On the floor behind the driver's seat were a pair of three inch black and white zebra printed leather heels.

Gabby stands with both hands on her waist as she stares at the car then at Josiah's home and back to the car. A million questions begin to run through her head causing her forehead to wrinkle. She knocks at the door one last time, still no answer. She decides to leave well enough alone and go on about her day just as it seems he has.

As she walks to the Gas station a couple blocks away to wait for a taxi, the strangest feeling began to form in her chest. It tightens while small knives jab at her heart. Her breathing speeds up as she slows down.

Falling into the wall of the gas station Gabby bends over grabbing her knees while panting. The tears start to flow uncontrollably. Now sitting on the ground she rests her hands in her face.

What is this, she asks herself.

Finally home, Gabby prepares a dinner of spinach salad with pan seared Tilapia. After dinner, she reads a bit of scripture then heads to bed. Unable to sleep from this evening's findings in the car parked at Josiah's house, she tosses and turns.

Lord, I believe when you said you would never leave nor forsake me…I need you now. You said that all things work for the good of those who love you but I feel like everything I have done in an attempt to try and do right has come back to bite me. I didn't kill the baby, so why do people make me feel like I did? I don't think I deserve any of this. Help me understand… Amen.

Gabby's eyes glued to the ceiling she lays awake all night expecting to get her understanding before day break.

OPPORTUNITY

Barely making it into the office this morning Gabby sits at her desk zipping through emails to ensure she hasn't missed any briefings. She usually arrives at least forty-five minutes early so that she feels completely in the know once her day starts.

Gabby squints at the caller ID as her phone rings on her desk.

"Gabby Fawn" she answers, uncertain of who's calling.

The call was about an event that had originated in Georgia but was looking to pick-up filming in Illinois.

The caller explains they have photographers as well as a filming crew, but got such great reviews on Gabby's editing and was willing to cancel their editor for this project to try her out.

Gabby, although delighted with the news, was also worried about the sacrifice of the commitment.

"Now this will require a lot, if not all, of your time. We shoot non-stop for about a month and would need editing turn around to be twenty-four to forty-eight hours.

Gabby sits back in her chair thinking over the offer. She was not too familiar with the state of Illinois and had only been once for her sister's graduation from University of Illinois-Springfield. This would also be a great opportunity to try and reconnect with her sister Gina since they haven't spoken in years.

"If you don't mind, I would like to take the weekend to process the information given, check my upcoming schedule and give you a well thought out answer. How's next week? Tuesday?

After going over a few more details of the job, the caller kindly grants Gabby the time and expresses her sincerity in looking forward to her response.

Martini's and tiny dresses…tonight? A text message from Tasha is displayed across Gabby's cell phone screen as it vibrates on her desk.

This Friday night feels different for Gabby. They haven't connected over the last couple weeks but this particular Friday stands out to her and she now reflects on how, for the last several months, her Friday evenings consisted of Josiah, watching a Netflix movie, preparing a meal that was randomly chosen out of a cookbook or simply snuggling and reading with each other.

As Gabby stuffs her few needed items (ID, money and lip gloss) into her gold sequin clutch, she thinks about what Josiah is doing tonight.

One last check of her hair in the mirror and she heads out the door for Martini's in her tiny gold dress.

"Great minds think alike!" Verna yells while embracing her matching friend.

Without previous planning, Gabby and Verna managed to step out in the exact same dress.

"I certainly hope no one mistakes me for a whore," Gabby jokes with Verna.

"Oh honey…it would require more than a dress to obtain my talents and be good at what I do," Verna Jokes back.

Tasha surprises the ladies by wearing a vibrant red mini-dress. She is not too big on color.

"I like," Verna takes Tasha by the hand and spins her around.

"We look like a doo-wop singing group," Gabby laughs.

The ladies agree in laughter as they enter the venue to enjoy a much needed girl's night out.

Dancing and laughing all night with the ladies is just what Gabby needed to get back into her normal head space. Josiah had become a part of that head space so it was only natural to still have him at the forefront of her mind by the end of the night.

"You crushed so many men in there Gabby. I know what you're going through and you want everything to work out with Josiah, but it feels good to know you still got it, right?" Tasha smiles at Gabby.

LATE NIGHTS, EARLY MORNINGS

Gabby rarely drives but tonight she took Storm, her black on black drop-top BMW out with her. After parting ways with the ladies she turns up some jazz and drives the speed limit down the highway, the opposite way from home. Gabby was enjoying the night air and the freedom of being at peace.

She pulls over near a park that is filled only with the glow of the surrounding street lights.

She closes her eyes and listens to the different insects buzzing around and the hooting of the owls in the tall trees. She smiles, thinking of her and Josiah sitting on the park bench laughing and talking as they have always been able to, until now.

Gabby reaches for her phone and places a call to Josiah, feeling confident that he would answer at this hour.

The phone rang three times and Gabby begins to think it was silly to call now knowing he may be asleep, but she got an answer. Just not the answer she was expecting.

"Hello."

A woman's voice comes through the other end but Gabby is unable to place it. She looks at the time on the screen in her car, 2:53am.

"Hello…" The voice says again but Gabby seems to have lost her words.

She quickly tries to run through the list of women in Josiah's life that she has met but could come up with nothing.

"I must have the wrong number," Gabby replies in a certain tone.

"You must," the woman responds and hangs up.

Gabby had a decision to make. Go over to Josiah's house and beat on the door until he answers or the neighbors call the police or go home and go to sleep.

The morning sun kisses Gabby's face as it peeks through the blinds she was too tired to close when she got in earlier this morning. She looks at the time: 10:00am. She stretches, pleased with her decision to come home. She may have been stretching in a little cell downtown had she not.

She looks through her outgoing calls to see if it had by chance all been a dream. Realizing it wasn't, she places a call that she thought she wasn't ready to.

"Hello, this is Gabby Fawn. I spoke with you regarding the trial editing position yesterday. I have made a decision sooner than I thought. I will be more than happy to take on the challenge and gain the experience. Please contact me back during the week to discuss further details."

CHAPTER 5

FROM THE TOP

FROM THE TOP

The cool of the night soothes Josiah as he lays out in his father's back yard on the hammock that had been there since he was a boy. He would run out there to clear his mind whenever his mother would leave him to go be with her other family.

"Come on in here Jo, your dinner is getting cold."

Josiah sits up slowly and stares over at the sliding glass door where Valerie, his mother, was standing. She is just as pretty as she was when he was a little boy.

Her teeth are just as pearly white and her long hair, although now sprinkled with gray, still shines bright as it blows in the night's wind.

"Yes ma'am, just clearing my head."

Josiah stops and gives his mother a soft kiss on the forehead as he passes by her into the kitchen. There at the table was Winston and his fiancé, Arin, looking through a wedding book Arin picked up at the library earlier that day to go over ideas for the reception.

Josiah's heart smiles as he watches his best friend hold his lady and smile while making wedding plans.

He is truly happy to be a part of this time in Winston's life but he doesn't care to show his joy for them outwardly at the moment. Although he declined Winston's offer for him to be his best man, Josiah didn't want to be completely absent so he chose to be present in planning and absent emotionally.

"Will Gabby be interested in joining the wedding party? I would love for her to be a bridesmaid," Arin says, spinning the wedding book around to point out a mint green bridesmaid dress with hints of gold around the straps.

Josiah laughs a gentle laugh as he pulls the book to himself for a closer look.

"Gabby hates the color green…yes, let's make her part of your wedding party!"

The room fills with laughter which is what Josiah was going for. Now they can't possibly hear the sadness in his joking attempt to make Gabby a part of this moment.

His mother saw right through the attempt Josiah was making to act as though everything was okay. She remembered that face and could see the nine year old boy who would stand on the front steps waving as she put her suitcase in the car to go play house elsewhere.

"Mommy always returns to you Jo. Chin up and let me see the man in you," she would say just before leaving him. He had no choice but to stand there, smile and wave as though he was okay with it. He wasn't, and all the years she left, she knew it.

"Jo, come sit over here and talk to me." Josiah's mother grabs him by the hand and leads him to the swing on the back porch.

Josiah pulls his hand away gently and rests it on her shoulder.

"Look Valerie, this is all still very fresh and new, don't push it. Let's start slow." The tears that fill his mother's eyes tell him that he failed let her down gently as he had planned.

"Valerie? I am your mother Josiah. No matter how you feel about my past and the choices I made in it, you must respect me as your mother. If you must refer to me as Valerie, I would rather not be referred to at all."

She wipes her tears as she pushes past her son.

Just as he would when Josiah was a boy, his father runs behind his mother to console her. Leaving Josiah feeling abandoned yet again.

What about me and my feelings? Just because I am a man doesn't mean I don't feel… Josiah thinks to himself as he stands staring into the night sky. He finds himself longing for Gabby's touch.

Josiah sits waiting around for the speech from his father that usually follows a fall out between him and his mother. But they never come out of the room. He contemplates initiating amends but it didn't feel genuine. He grabs his plate, which was cold as his mother told him it would be and went back to the hammock where he knew he could find peace to get through the night.

TOO MANY iPHONES

An alarm buzzes piercing through Josiah's sound sleep earlier than he had wanted. He sits up and looks over at Arin who is all dressed up in running gear, stretching at the door.

"Sorry to wake you. I am usually on the road by the time my alarm sounds…guess I'm a bit slow this morning. Gotta be in shape for the big day," she smiles and darts out the front door.

Josiah wanders through his father's house looking for his phone. It has been six days since he made the choice to not look at it trying not to be anxious for Gabby's call.

He enters his father's room where he had slept the first night he arrived as he remembers putting it on the nightstand.

Instead of his phone, he finds his mother and father going at it like it was 1975 again and they were madly in love.

"Excuse me! I am so sorry!" Josiah laughs and quickly closes the door.

"You didn't know he could still get down like that huh?" Winston was laughing with Josiah at the end of the hall. "Good morning man, that was certainly alarming!" Winston pats Josiah on the back as they go to sit on the sofa.

"Hey man, there are too many iPhones in one house. Yours just so happened to get me cussed out."

Winston hands the now dead cell phone to Josiah and continues, "Funny story, your phone was next to my wallet in Jimmy's bedroom where Arin was showering and getting dressed. You know momma had the guest bathroom on lock with getting herself dressed and ready for Sunday service and all, she had the makeup and the--"

"Come on man, stay on track." Josiah interrupts, pulling Winston back on topic, Josiah's phone.

"Yeah, so…the phone rang and Arin answered, you know, because she thought it was mine. On the other end was Gabby but she didn't even pay attention to the screen where her picture and name pops up so she didn't know! Arin storms out the room and charges at me while I'm sitting and playing dominoes with Uncle Rob and Jimmy. That woman is such a hot head sometimes but boy do I love her."

Winston wraps up his long winded story smiling at the thought of his hot head fiancé.

"Why am I just now getting my phone, and dead?" Josiah becomes angry.

Winston begins explaining but Josiah had no patience to listen. He needs to find his phone charger so that he can see how many messages Gabby must have left in anger.

A few minutes of searching and he gives up. During the search he was thinking about what he would say if he was to call her back, what he would say if she didn't answer. He decides there is nothing to say.

"Here baby, is this what you were looking for?" Valerie stands before Josiah in his father's robe with the charger he had been searching for in hand.

"Thank you." He grabs the charger and extends his hand toward the sofa to sit hoping she would talk a moment.

She sits, patting the cushion beside her for him to join her.

"When you called me and asked me to come to your home, I was overjoyed. My attempts to spend time with you in the past were all out of guilt, and you felt that so I respect your choice to keep your distance."

Valerie places one hand on her son's knee and the other on his face.

"I have always loved you Josiah. You are my little chocolate drop. I am proud of the man that you have become and whether you knew it or not, whether you seen me or not, I was always there. I watched you walk across the stage to receive your diploma, even though I didn't get an invite. I was even there when you received both your degrees. Son, I have always been in the shadow, waiting for you to want me. I understand if you don't need me."

Josiah places a finger on his mother's lips. Tears fall from his eyes as he begins to share his heart regarding her.

"I knew you were there…and you were there because you knew I needed you. I did and I do."

Josiah rests his head in his mother's lap and she rubs his back as her tears begin to fall. There was energy between them that neither had ever felt. They realize in this moment that for their own selfish reasons they never allowed themselves to connect.

Arin walks in, unaware of the magic that was happening in Jimmy's living room.

"Momma Val, I need the keys to your Camry, I left my gym bag in there so I had to run this morning in old gear I left in Winston's trunk a few weeks ago. I feel so gross."

She laughs, but briefly. She now sees the tears in both her soon to be in-law's eyes.

Backing up slowly she apologizes and assures Valerie the things in her car can wait.

"Son, can we agree to not look back? Can we just move forward? I know there is hurt in your heart and most, if not all, is because of me but I don't want that to hinder the future from this point."

Josiah sits up and looks intensely in his mother's eyes, grabbing her hands he breaks the question that he knew would cause her to feel a little uncomfortable.

"I was thinking we could try family counseling." Josiah says in an uncertain tone.

She and his father were very old school in that they didn't believe in talking with outsiders about inside issues.

Valerie rises up from the sofa and grabs hold of her son's hands. Her tears now dried up, she gives Josiah the same intense stare he had given her.

"Now, you're asking a lot Josiah."

He shifts in his seat knowing she is upset because he went from *son* to *Josiah*.

"I can't make any promises…but please be okay with knowing I am trying."

She walks out of the room, leaving Josiah with his disappointment yet again.

ILLINOIS

Rushing to gather all her last minute items Gabby races from each corner of her condo grabbing everything she thinks she will need while in Illinois. Running the list down in her head she realizes she is forgetting one thing. But it was at the office which she dreaded going back to.

When she broke the news to Victor about the project, he had many words for Gabby, none of which were kind.

"What the hell am I supposed to do for an entire month without you here doing your part Gabby? I have the mind to tell you to not even return once your little project is over. What do you think about that?" Victor asked firmly.

Gabby didn't satisfy him with a response. She simply gathered what she thought was all she needed and went on her way.

Gabby is, and always has been, confident with her position with the company and Victor knew that. He likes to try and push buttons that Gabby never has functioning.

The Taxi arrives thirty minutes later than Gabby had been promised. Luckily she was too focused on her mission to get to the airport on time to have a fit.

"I need you to make two stops, is that alright?"

Gabby hands the driver a crisp twenty dollar bill after he closes the trunk on her over stuffed luggage.

"Certainly, ma'am," the driver accepts and opens the back door for Gabby to climb in.

En route to destination one, Gabby's phone rings. She searches eagerly through her purse, her backpack and her briefcase, no cell phone. The caller continues to call back each time they were unanswered.

"We are here, ma'am," the taxi pulls up to her place of employment.

She looks up toward the twelfth floor.

It's noon, maybe everyone is out to lunch.

As the elevator doors open she smiles; just about everyone was out, just as she thought.

She hadn't been in the office for a couple of days but it already felt foreign to her. Opening the door to her office she discovers she had become foreign to them as well, her name plate was replaced.

Looking down at her watch she debates whether she has time to stay and get answers from Victor regarding her office.

"Your flight is in an hour, get out of there."

Gabby often calls on Tasha for some help with her decisions when her own head is a bit too cloudy to make good ones.

"That's just it, why wouldn't I be wanted anymore? Because I am trying new things to advance my career? He should be supportive of what I am doing. He didn't get to where he is just sitting on his oversized behind in an office all day…you know?"

Tasha laughs at her friend's frustration. She has known Gabby for many years which meant she knows when her friend is being ridiculous.

"Gab, you have a lot going on. Maybe you're over exaggerating, take a look around…someone has to be there to explain what's going on."

Gabby calms down. "Ok, I'll call you right back."

Racing through the office Gabby finds not one person that would have information.

"May I help you with something, Gabby?" One of the interns approaches who is just as annoying as newbie is to Gabby.

"Where are they all…where's Victor?" Gabby is unable to hide her frustration.

The intern leads Gabby to the main conference hall.

"By the way, congratulations." The intern says before leaving Gabby at the closed conference hall doors.

Gabby had the courage but there was no time for her to walk in or even knock. The door swings open and out walks Victor.

"Gabby, what are you doing back so soon? Have you changed your mind?" Victor wraps his heavy arm around Gabby's neck.

Disgusted, Gabby ducks down to get from beneath his arm and stands before him crossing hers. "What's the deal with my office Victor, why is your name plate on my desk?

"Walk with me." Victor attempts to place his arm around Gabby's neck once again until he notices the look on her face.

Gabby lets him lead the way.

Luckily Gabby's taxi driver is still patiently waiting for her downstairs after her quick chat with Victor filling her in on the changes at the office.

After several apologies, Gabby sinks into the back seat boggled down with more decisions than before she went in. The stop was simply for her on the go make-up kit which she recovered from the box marked *FLOOR 15* at the cube right outside her office where she once sat and reflected on her qualifications to even have an office.

"Ma'am, your device?"

The taxi driver hands Gabby her cell that had fallen underneath his seat.

Ignoring the missed call alert on the main screen she goes directly to contacts and searches for Josiah.

She drops the phone in her lap and throws her hands in the air as it dawns on her it probably wouldn't be the best idea to call him.

"It's so hard to break a habit. Good or bad, I called and told him everything…that is changing now." Gabby pours out to Tasha, finally calling her back.

"What happened in the office?" Tasha asks ignoring Gabby's late discovery of the change in her and Josiah's relationship.

She let's Tasha know she is almost to the airport and that she would call her as soon as she touches down in Illinois.

Almost two hours later she is awakened by the wheels of the plane hitting the runway. She looks beside her as she stretches; there is a young girl seemingly awaking from a slumber also.

Gabby smiles at the girl but she doesn't smile back. The little girl wears a look of worry that breaks Gabby's heart more and more the longer she studies her.

Reaching into her purse, Gabby searches for something that may put a smile on her face.

"Look what I found in my bag, do you like cherry flavor?" Gabby hands her a piece of candy that had been in her purse for some time now.

"Oh no, she doesn't need anything like that, big enough already." The lady sitting beside the little girl speaks up with a deep southern accent.

The look of worry becomes contagious, jumping onto Gabby's face.

After giving the woman with fire engine red hair, orange and white striped leggings and three inch gold stiletto heels the once over with her eyes, she puts the piece of candy back into her purse.

"I'm sorry, I don't think you should be calling her big, she is a child. I do apologize for offering her candy without asking you. That was wrong on my end."

Gabby gets up from her seat and removes her carry-on from the overhead and makes her way down the aisle. She didn't turn back to see if the little girl was watching her in fear that she was…with eyes that say help me.

GINA

"I think you are right, I need to speak with someone regarding how I truly feel about my past. The look in her eyes…" Gabby takes a pause in her confession to her mother.

"I can't help but wonder if my child has that same look on her face," she concludes.

Gabby hasn't openly spoken about the decision she made more than ten years ago with anyone. Not since the fall out with her sister after finding out she had lost yet another child.

"How dare you take a gift God has given you and just pass it to the next person whom you don't even know. Just disrespect God and his decision to bless you," Gina screamed at Gabby from the hospital bed after learning of her seventh miscarriage.

"How dare you judge me? You don't know how hard it was to make the choice I did. You're so selfish you wouldn't even care about that baby being somewhere else had you been able to carry your own. Maybe that's why you can't carry your own…too worried about everyone else and their life."

Once words leave your mouth and someone's ears catch them, you can't take them back. Gabby touches her neck remembering how her throat felt of flames after those words came out. She looks in the mirror and sees past her reflection to that day, the look on her sister's face burned her heart just as it had all those years ago. It's when she knew their relationship was broken.

"Sincerity is found in the eyes, forgiveness resides there also. If I was you, I would seek to find what is in hers." Her mother suggests.

After settling into the suite, compliments of the network, Gabby takes the advice her mother gave as they spoke on the ride from the airport.

She knew that if she was going to take her mother's advice she would have to dress for battle. She put on her black leggings, white tank covered with a classic jean jacket. Tied up her Skecher walking shoes and finished her battle gear off with placing a Gophers baseball cap on her head.

Finishing off her bottle of water she sits in the bay window looking out for her taxi to arrive. She had heard rumors of the taxi services not being on time in Chicago but that was not bothersome to her as she dealt with the same issue in Atlanta.

Looking around the suite, she grows anxious and decides to go wait at the hotel entrance.

A chill comes over her as she goes to exit the room. Her heart tells her she isn't fully dressed so she searches through her backpack for the rest of her gear. She finds the case and quickly opens it up.

Ephesians 6:11-17 Put on all of God's armor so that you will be able to stand firm against all tragedies and tricks of the devil. For we are not fighting against people made of flesh and blood, but against the evil rulers and authorities of the unseen world, against those mighty powers of darkness who rule this world, and against wicked spirits in the heavenly realms. Use every piece of God's armor to resist the enemy in the time of evil, so that after the battle you will still be standing firm. Stand your ground putting on the sturdy belt of truth and the body armor of God's righteousness. For shoes, put on the peace that comes from the Good News, so that you will be fully prepared. In every battle you will need faith as your shield to stop the fiery arrows aimed at you by Satan. Put on salvation as your helmet and take the sword of the spirit, which is the word of God.

Just as she reads the last verse, her phone buzzes and an Illinois number displays on her screen. Certain it is the taxi driver, she grabs her room key off the breakfast bar and begins her journey to where she hopes is a happy place.

The ride to Joliet from the city feels like forever to Gabby as she sits in the back of the taxi making mental notes of what needs to be said once she arrives at her destination. She thinks about how she had prepared so well for her talk with Josiah that never happened because he never showed up and was hoping this didn't end up the same way…painful, confusing and unresolved.

As the cab pulls in to the community, Gabby sits up and stares out of the window in amazement. Every yard was well manicured the homes were very grand and there was no movement aside from the wind that blew fiercely today.

The driver pulls into the lot of a three story brick home with double doors, beige with gold trimmed design in the glass.

Gabby looks at the text message her mother sent with the address, *44237 Staples Circle,* and then back at the house. The golden numbers over the garage door say this is the right place.

Gabby steps out of the taxi feeling ready to face her past in an attempt to move forward into a better future. She had decided before even boarding the plane to not let her emotions take over at any time.

"Seek to understand rather than be understood," her mother's voice was clear in her mind.

Gabby takes two deep breaths and knocks on the door of the beautiful home. She squints a bit trying to see through the designs on the glass, anxious to see if a butler or maid approaches as she had made up in her mind would.

A minute passes but no one appears to be making their way to the door. She skims the border of the doors searching for a doorbell but she doesn't see one. What she does see is a camera that had been watching her the entire time. Now nervous she steps back off the stairs and observes the home more closely.

She spots another camera above the garage doors and on the roof on either side. Shaking her head, she takes one last look at the door before going back to the taxi which she asked to stand by in case she was turned away.

As she made her way around the pink flowered bushes aligning the front of the home, she hears the doors open. She looks back and there Gina stood and, at no surprise to Gabby, without a smile.

"Oh how disappointing. You look nothing at all as I remember you. What is it you need? Fallen on hard times?"

CHAPTER 6

ROLLING THE DICE

ROLLING THE DICE

Phone finally charged, Josiah stares at it contemplating his next move.

What do I have to lose? She either answers and hangs up or doesn't answer...not too bad. He convinces himself.

In need of a little more time before making a decision, Josiah decides to shower and freshen up his body as well as his mind.

Allowing the water to heat up, Josiah stands staring at his reflection as steam begins filling the bathroom.

He rubs his neck and rolls his head around slowly, trying to loosen his muscles. Now relaxed in the upper portion of his body he realizes his muscle below the belt needs to release some tension. He closes his eyes and remembers the passion between himself and Gabby. He imagines cupping her firm behind and pulling her into him. He could hear her moans clear in his mind and feel her legs wrapped around his waist.

A knock at the door cuts into his moment.

"Are you riding over to Ms. Briggs for brunch, son," his father inquires.

Josiah confirms he will be in attendance and hops into the shower.

As he buttons the last button on his lavender and white dress shirt he notices the red light flashing on his phone; there is a message.

"Hey man, I need to access some of your client files while you're away. Call me back or text me the cabinet code," Claude requested over voicemail.

Holding his phone reminds him he needs to call Gabby and explain the mix-up with Arin.

As the line rings Josiah fills up with great anxiety. Ring...ring...ring...

Finally there was an answer but a hello didn't follow. He could hear breathing on the other end so he knew she had to be on the line and was just waiting for him to beg for forgiveness…he did.

"Baby, I am so sorry. Please let me explain to you what happened when you called, It's really silly and I pray to God we can laugh about it later."

Josiah is interrupted by Gabby's sobbing.

"Now is not a good time for apologies. Yes, we have a lot to deal with when it comes to us and what we need to do with this relationship. Right now I just need a friend."

Gabby takes a deep breath and freely allows the tears to fall. She is thinking very heavy on the incident with her sister.

"I am headed to a family gathering now. I can come by once we're done so we can talk."

Not wanting Josiah to know she is not in town at the moment, she tells him to just give a call back once he is done with his family.

"I have quite a few things to do today myself," she lies.

Josiah returns Claude's call, providing what he had requested over voicemail. He also provided him with a truth that he wasn't sure he was ready for, let alone his business partner.

"I am taking a break from this whole thing, man. I don't feel much like advising people on their finances at the moment. I need to be advised on my life."

Stunned, Claude was less concerned with the advisement of his life and more concerned about the future of the business they had built together.

"What does that mean, exactly? You have taken too much time away as it is. Where are you going with this?"

Deciding he is not ready to address Claude's questions, Josiah responds with a vague, "I'll keep you posted."

FAMILIAR FACES

Although Gabby's assignment didn't start for a couple of days, she thought that she would come right in mending the relationship between her and Gina but, she now knows, it is going to take more than a couple of days.

After dining downstairs in the hotel's restaurant, Gabby climbs into the king size bed and wraps herself up in the fresh white linen.

Grabbing her purse off the nightstand she digs around for something to help her sleep. She pulls out a picture of her and Josiah from their first date at the steakhouse and places it on the nightstand and reaches back into her purse for a little more visual comfort. She removes a black and white but it didn't display much of an image.

She places the black and white picture on the pillow beside her, gently dusting it off with her fingers as it had been in the bottom of her purse for some time.

"Look, I need your help. I haven't spoken to you in a while because, I guess, all this time I had been doing fine. You know me pretty well. How do you think I should handle this whole situation with Gina? Will she ever forgive me? You have, so, how on earth could she not?"

Gabby hits the bed hard with her fist trying to release some frustration. She looks over to make sure the picture is still in place.

"I just want this all to be over. I just want us all to be happy. I know that's what you want, too. So tell me, how do I deal with this?"

She continues on as she sank down into the bed and rests her head on the pillow beside the picture.

A single tear falls from her eye and, just like that, she finds sleep.

Awakened by a loud knock, Gabby jumps up and out of the large bed.

"Housekeeping!"

Looking over at the clock on the wall, Gabby wipes her eyes and shakes her head. Taking another look, now that the sleep is out of her eyes, she is shocked that she had slept past noon.

"Sure, come on in," she welcomes the two Hispanic women entering the room, holding the door open for them.

Splashing water on her face, she tries to wake up from her long slumber. Pulling her hair into a bun at the top of her head she decides to throw on some active gear and take a quick jog around the city as she had seen some women out doing yesterday. *It looked refreshing*, she thought.

"Your ultrasound ma'am?"

The short Hispanic lady with shoulder length jet black hair was standing directly in front of Gabby holding her black and white picture which she had a conversation with last night to her face.

Gabby snatches the picture from her hand.

"What are you doing with this? Don't go in my things! Just clean the room."

Gabby storms past her to put that picture, along with the picture of her and Josiah, away in the top drawer of the night stand.

"No, no ma'am! I find on floor." The lady points in a panic at the floor next to the bed.

Ignoring her efforts to rectify the situation, Gabby walks out the room not giving the lady another look.

Two miles in her jog, Gabby decides it's time to head back to the room and get ready for the day, even though she has no clue what the day will consist of at this point.

While taking a moment to stretch before getting back to it, she slowly inhales the crisp morning air while she looks around admiring the city's beautiful roughness.

"Excuse me, are you familiar with this area," a young girl asks, tapping on Gabby's shoulder.

Standing straight up, Gabby shakes her head "no". She had every intention to say no but the word couldn't make its way past her lips.

She was caught off guard by this young girl's eyes; they look so familiar to her. She stood shoulder to shoulder with Gabby and had long curly, red hair and a face full of red freckles.

The young girl wore a smile when she first approached Gabby but it starts fading as she stands there watching the woman stare.

"Ok, thank you," the girl slowly walks around Gabby and continues on her way.

Gabby turns to watch the young girl walk away. Thankful for the bench nearby, Gabby takes a seat and ends up sitting in that same place for an hour wondering why the young girl stood out to her.

Shortly after Gabby arrives back in her room and settles her phone rang.

"How are things in the windy city, girly," Tasha inquires.

Gabby sits and shares with Tasha all that has happened since she arrived.

"Girl, you are trying to put too much on yourself at once. You need to get into the groove of your assignment and the city, and then dive into your family drama."

Gabby felt her friend was giving good advice but she was just not in the mood to take it.

ANOTHER TRY

Gina opens the door wearing a painted on smile. After Gabby called crying and pleading Gina agreed to sit down and speak about their differences.

She leads Gabby into a grand dining area. The windows dressed with beautiful gold and cream paisley printed curtains and bound midway with thick gold rope. The table which seated ten was marble with taupe leather high back chairs. Large paintings of scenery hang on the cream textured walls and ancient Greek statues stood in each corner of the space.

"Have a seat," Gina extends her hand toward the two Victorian style chairs in one corner of the grand room.

Gabby sits slowly and watches as Gina sits quickly in the seat beside her. Though the chairs were separated by a small glass table Gabby feels they may need a little more space between them than that.

Silence had the floor as the sisters looked everywhere but at each other. Both had their legs crossed and feet twitching, indicating nervousness.

"Remember when daddy brought home that cute little black lab. He came in the house cradling it in his arms and said, you girls ready for this type of responsibility? You and I, all full of excitement and joy, both shouted that we were," Gina began.

Not looking for a response, she smirks and lowers her head as she continues her story.

"Daddy stood and looked at us both, hands outstretched to receive the puppy… He handed it to you and asked, 'What shall we call him?'"

Gabby cleared her throat and sat up in her seat as she thought back to that Sunday afternoon. She remembers the story but not quite that way. Gabby knew the entire story.

She had been sick with the flu for an entire week, her father came into her bedroom one night and asked what would make her feel better.

"A doggy, daddy. He will lick away my flu…won't he?"

Her father patted her on the head and tucked her in for the night. She didn't know that she would really get a puppy. From what Gabby could remember, just talking about a puppy made her feel better.

Gina went on with story after story of how Gabby was always presented with gifts first and given so much responsibility that she wasn't ready for.

"On my wedding day, daddy told me that you were going to make a beautiful bride one day…you Gabby."

Gina doesn't bother wiping the tears that were falling from her eyes like a raging waterfall or even the snot that was running over her lips.

"I named the dog Chips, Gina…Chips!" Gabby kneels before her sister and reaches for her hand. "That should have been the moment you knew I would need you in my life to help me make better decisions as my big sister. There are many stories I can think of where you got something that I wanted and felt it wasn't fair but what good would telling those stories do us today?"

Gabby's tears begin to collect in the corners of her eyes. Gina notices and jumps out of her seat.

"Please don't cry on this. It's silk."

Gabby watches her sister in disgust as she runs out of the grand dining room.

"Damn," Gabby says aloud as she gathers herself from the floor and begins pacing back and forth waiting for Gina to return.

After about ten minutes Gabby peeks her head out of the dining room and down the hall to her right then looks over at the kitchen on the left. Gina was nowhere within her site.

Gabby walks into the kitchen, running her finger across the large marble topped island in the center of the room. She stops and imagines herself on a cooking show for a moment.

"Today, we will show you how to prepare…Pizza!" She says through her smile in what she thought to be an Italian accent.

"I remember that…we loved cook time with daddy." Gina, also smiling, stands in the entryway as she begins down memory lane with Gabby.

Gabby comes from around the island and walks to her sister who she embraces with a firm hug.

No longer worried about her silk house dress, Gina allows her own tears to fall as she embraces her little sister.

"Walton will be home soon, he's not really into surprise guests…" Gina clears her throat.

"How about you return tomorrow and we prepare lunch on camera just like we use to with daddy?" Gina continued.

Gabby is delighted with her sister's offer to have bonding time but she can't help but notice how her body language changed and her eyes began shifting when she mentioned her husband Walton.

"It's a date!" Gabby confirms as she is lead to the door. She wants to ask but knows it's too soon to pry into her sister's personal life.

SURPRISE GUESTS

By week's end Gabby is over her decision to take a chance and try something new in her career. Everyone she works with directly is cold and rude, and she doesn't even have any support to go home to or go out with.

Lunch plans fell through with Gina earlier in the week and although they talk everyday on the phone, Gabby felt like she needed to spend time with someone…she misses her friends and longs for her and her sister to get closer.

"It's Friday night, get ready to hit your favorite spot while we keep the music coming." 107.5fm WGCI keeps her company as she flips through an Essence magazine she picked up on her way in.

With a half day shoot starting early in the morning Gabby decides to call it a night so that she can be bright eyed and bushy tailed for her side eyed, hard tail co-workers.

As she fluffs her pillow, her phone vibrates on the end table. She looks at the clock which told her it was entirely too early for a phone call.

Not even bothering to look at the screen to see who is calling, she puts the phone to her ear.

"Yeah," she says in as clear of a voice as she could muster up.

"It's Friday night and you sleep? Get up girl, we almost there!"

Gabby pushes the phone a little closer to her ear.

"Verna?" Gabby rolls over and looks up at the ceiling.

"And Tash! We in the Chi, boo!" Tasha chimes in.

Gabby begins laughing hysterically while looking at the clock again.

Only my friends would catch a plane in the middle of the night to go out in a different city, Gabby thinks to herself while anxiously waiting for her girlfriends' arrival at about 3am.

Tasha and Verna join Gabby for breakfast at the restaurant across the street from the hotel.

"Why didn't we just order room service?" Verna complains as she straightens the scarf that was wrapped around her head.

Tasha and Gabby laugh together at Verna's complaining.

"Where's all that energy from last night? You were all ready to hit the town just a few hours ago," Tasha reminds her.

The waiter approaches the table in a white cotton button down shirt, black slacks and a red apron tied around his waist. He appeared to be very well built underneath his shirt and Verna wanted him to know she noticed.

"Work out much?" She smiles at him.

"I'm sorry ma'am, what was that?" The waiter asked genuinely unaware of Verna's comment/question.

"Where is your name badge, aren't you required to wear one?" Gabby jumps in trying to prevent her friend from embarrassing the kind young man waiting on them.

"I asked if you work out much dear, I am admiring your build...under that shirt."

Verna smiles again, only this time it was a *do you understand now* smile.

"Jamison, my name is Jamison," he laughs, exposing his perfectly straight, amazingly white teeth. "No, we are not required to wear a name tag, but if that is something you feel the owner should consider, I will be more than happy to suggest it to him next time he is in town."

Impressed, Gabby nods approvingly at the young man and told him she would like that very much.

A now irritated Verna clears her throat and sits straight up in her seat. No longer interested in the waiter Verna asks, "The owner, what does he look like?"

Laughter finds Jamison again as he tells the ladies he will give them a few more minutes to decide on orders.

"Victor wants to promote me," Gabby cuts into the laughter with her serious tone.

Tasha looks over at Verna waiting for a response, she already knew about the offer presented to Gabby.

"Promote you to what? Run the entire company? Hell...about time! You already do," Verna begins to laugh but quickly realizes she was the only one cheerful.

"Victor explained that me taking this opportunity made him realize I am not afraid to step out of my comfort zone to get a job done and that I am open to new things. He filled me in on some company changes...people will be transferred."

Gabby searches her friend's face for reaction but there was just a blank stare.

"Gabby has been given the opportunity to advance her career and run the new office opening in Los Angeles. She is basically going to be the Victor of LA," Tasha jumps in, wanting it to get out faster than Gabby was allowing.

Verna's stare quickly went from blank to wicked.

"Why the hell does she have all the information Gab?"

Gabby, now sharing the wicked stare toward Tasha, decides she doesn't want to ruin this time with her friends, especially since they just arrived.

"Girl, let's talk about all this later…I have to get to my shoot."

The ladies finish breakfast and Gabby invites them to come along to her morning shoot, ensuring them it was only going to last a couple of hours. The ladies knew what Gabby's career was but never had the opportunity to see firsthand.

Seven hours later Tasha is a co-producer and Verna is a professional set whore. She has flirted around with all the male extras and collected the numbers of the leading men.

"There were only four of them Gabby, stop looking at me like that." Verna's guilty conscience makes her lash out at Gabby as she walks past her to collect the fourth and final number.

Gabby smiles, happy to have the support of her friends in this foreign place in the world, as well as this foreign place in her life.

She fills her stainless steel coffee mug with orange juice and sips slowly as she observes her surrounding and reflects on the blessings in her life.

Pulling her phone from her back pocket, she scrolls through the contacts until she reaches the name of who she believes is one of the many blessings in her life.

"How soon can you make it to Illinois?"

CHAPTER 7

UNCOVERED

UNCOVERED

There are many pictures along the walls of the house; mostly black and white pictures from Gina's wedding ceremony and odd angled black and whites of different buildings from around the world.

Gabby comes to an opening of what looks like a long hallway leading to stairs. On the walls of this hallway are many pictures of a child, a little boy who looked to be about five or six years old.

She stops and closely observes each picture looking for some kind of clue to tell her who this little boy is.

At the end of the hall at the top of the stairs there is a picture of Gina and Walton holding an infant whom Gabby assumes is the little boy from all the other pictures.

Looking down the stairs she wonders what is down there.

The light from the opening of the hallway only reaches so far before it goes black.

Gabby decides to take a step and ends up missing it, sliding down into the closed door.

"Gabby...?"

She hears Gina calling and quickly runs back to the top of the stairs and walks quickly toward the opening of the hallway while rubbing her, now sore, behind.

"I was just admiring the black and white photos here. Have you taken up photography?"

"There is no need for foolish lies. I can clearly see what you were up to...snooping!" Gina grows angry.

Realizing Gina is about to trip, Gabby decides not to join her.

"Gina please, if I am snooping I have the right to…all I am doing is trying to figure out who you are."

Gina crosses her arms and gives Gabby a blank look.

"We are sisters that grew up under the same roof, provided with the same love and discipline."

Gabby moves closer to her sister to read her straight on.

"What you hold against me is not my fault. Your inability to carry a child is between you and God and last I checked He makes no mistakes. Instead of blaming me or anyone else, ask God why he made you this way and how you can use it for His glory."

Gina begins to giggle and soon after laughs a loud laugh.

"I am trying here Gab…that's a lot more than you know right now. What are you doing, exactly?"

Gabby walks toward Gina but each step Gabby takes forward Gina takes back.

After an hour of trying to reason with her, Gabby considers throwing in the towel. They hear the alarm chime which alerts them that the front door was ajar.

The look on Gina's face startles Gabby. Gina is clearly caught off guard.

"Baby love, look who I brought home today," Walton's voice echoes through the house.

Immediately after Walton's announcement, Gabby hears little feet running up the stairs.

He steps into the kitchen with a surprised look on his face.

"Didn't know we had guests. There are no cars in the lot," Walton extends his hand to Gabby.

"Hello Walton. I know it's been some time but the formal handshake is not necessary."

Gabby's eyes shift between her sister and her husband.

The awkward silence is broken by the sound of feet now running down the stairs.

Gabby staring anxiously at the kitchen entry way, feels her heart beating out of her chest.

"Mums, Mums…" a young child cries out.

The little boy from the pictures had come to life. He was standing right in front of Gabby with the sweetest little face and eyes that appeared more familiar than ones she had just seen in pictures.

"I ride the plane…vroooom" The little boy explains to Gina who not once took her eyes off Gabby.

"I think a car goes vroom little buddy, don't you think?" Gabby slowly drops down to one knee and reaches for the boy.

As she extends her arms she notices her watch reads a quarter to five and she needs to be on her way to the airport.

"My name is Gabby, what's yours?" Arms still extended Gabby tries to draw the boy in.

He smiles and grabs onto Gina's leg.

"Hi." He says bashfully.

Gina pulls the young boy off her leg and pushes him toward her sister.

"That is Aunt Gabby. Go give her a hug, Prince."

He runs to Gabby's arms and she embraces him firmly.

"Prince, your name is Prince?" She asks while running her fingers through his curly sandy brown almost reddish hair.

He gives a nodding confirmation while pulling himself from her arms. Walton takes him by the hand leading him and leaving the sisters together once again.

"He's beautiful...who is he Gina?"

Gabby realizes not much was going to come from Gina's mouth, at least not right now. She shows herself out with every intention to come back.

AT IT AGAIN

Skimming through the flight times posted on the four large screens at the airport, Gabby grows impatient.

She fails to spot the flights coming in from Atlanta but all the flights said *ON TIME* so she found comfort in that.

"I believe the restrooms are to your left, ma'am."

The familiar voice spins Gabby right around and into the arms of Josiah who was laughing hysterically.

"The way you were rocking side to side, I was sure you needed to pee...I know it couldn't be excitement," he chuckles.

Despite his failed attempt to humor her, Gabby is unable to let him go so she just holds tight for a while longer.

While on the shuttle heading to the pick-up area, both realize how awkward the last month or so has been between them. There was small talk but it just didn't feel like before.

"I have a great suite...you are welcome to stay in it with me. The production company is covering everything."

Josiah smiles and reaches for Gabby's hand to hold. She pulls away.

"On second thought, you're right...you should just see if you can get a room on the same floor."

Now back at the hotel, Gabby places her bag on the bar stool near the door of her suite and climbs up into the one next to it. Though it was not the comfort of her own condo, she was happy to be in what was, for the time being, home.

Laying her head down on her arms she takes a deep breath.

Once Josiah secured a room down the hall she told him she would check in on him after she gets some rest. She explained that she had been working like crazy.

By week's end Gabby and Josiah feel familiar again. Many late nights filled with laughter and 'remember when's' brought them right to where they left off.

"I know that wasn't some woman you were seeing that answered your phone. I was just dealing with so much, I guess I wanted to…needed to be mad at someone."

Josiah wraps his arms around Gabby and squeezes tight as they inhale the crisp morning air on the balcony of Gabby's suite. He places a kiss on the top of her head.

"I want nothing more than for you to trust me, Gabby. I will never put myself in a position to hurt you."

Gabby knows he is telling the truth and she lets him know by turning to him and planting a kiss on his full smooth lips.

That one kiss turns into multiple and she straddles herself over him. Grabbing her waist he feels himself rise to the occasion but tries hard to fight the temptation.

Gabby's hormones were working overtime as she, too, tries to fight the temptation. Emotions that were pent up from weeks apart from each other were now leaking heavily from their fingertips with every touch, and their lips, with every kiss.

The heat building between their bodies grows hotter. Gabby's hips grind on Josiah and she feels his body responding.

A knock at the door allows them to regain lost control, as they scatter to pull themselves together, like teenagers making out under the hallway stairs when they hear someone coming down them.

"Here is your final cut, check out is in an hour. If you decide to stay beyond that, the network is not responsible for your expenses."

One of the producers was standing outside her door in an all red jumpsuit and black rubber boots. Her hand was extended toward Gabby and in it was a medium sized manila envelope that read *Final Check – G. Fawn*.

Gabby looks the producer over once more before closing the door.

A once horny Gabby lays to rest as the now confused Gabby awakens. She plops down on the sofa and begins to open the envelope.

"Maybe you should wait until you get home to open that." Josiah advises as he begins gathering the bags she had packed the night before and bringing them to the door.

Now returning to Atlanta, the unexpected five hour layover was causing Gabby to become anxious about the content in the manila envelope that her oddly dressed ex-coworker delivered that morning. It seemed like too much envelope for one little check. When Josiah was in the restroom, she broke her promise to hold off until she got home.

Now unable to hide her stress, Josiah reads every bit of it that's written across her face.

"Is everything alright?" He leans into her in an attempt to have a private conversation on this wide open plane and as he leans in he notices the opened manila envelope in the seat pocket in front of her.

Gabby repositions herself to face Josiah, takes a deep breath and begins to fill him in.

"I have a nephew…a five year old nephew." Anger begins to write itself across Gabby's face, replacing just a small portion of the stress already there.

"He is adorable! He has red hair and freckles…I have seen those features in every child I dream about."

Josiah now confused, but at the same time concerned, reaches for Gabby's hand which he discovers is trembling.

"My baby would be five now, you know…" Anger completely claims her face all at once, dismissing the other emotions trying to write themselves there.

Afraid Gabby was about to rip off a bandage that was covering an unhealed wound in the wrong place at the wrong time, Josiah quickly grabs Gabby, pulling her head into his chest as he shushes her.

"Rest now, talk later," he asks hopeful she will agree.

MAKING ROOM

A cheese omelet, fruit and a glass of orange juice are staring back at Gabby when she opens her eyes. She sits herself up in Josiah's comfortable king sized bed and begins to eat the fruit. She smiles at the thought of Josiah's kindness to have made her breakfast.

"Good morning, beautiful," Josiah appears fully dressed in fitness attire.

Gabby quickly pushes the navy blue down comforter to the side, "Wait, I'll run with you."

Disappointed, Gabby slowly covers herself back up after Josiah tells her he has already been out for his run.

"Gotta get up earlier than ten my dear," he smiles.

They chose to have the cab driver make one stop at Josiah's home last night; he only lives ten minutes from the airport so it made sense to call it a night there.

Gabby looks at all her luggage piled on top of each other in Josiah's closet and laughs. His once large walk-in closet now seemed so small.

"Could you imagine if I lived here?" She laughs out loud directing Josiah to the closet with a nod of her head.

He sits on the bed beside her and grabs her hand. "Yes, I can imagine that. In fact, I have been thinking about that lately," Josiah admits.

Gabby, now in tears from laughing so hard, pushes him to the side as she climbs out of the bed and runs to the closet.

"Ok, show me where I would fit?"

Josiah joins her in laughter as he approaches the opening of the closet where she was standing.

Again he grabs her hand, now placing it on his chest.

"There is always room in here; therefore space can surely be made in here," he extends his arm out to display his open home.

Laughter now at a minimum, Gabby begins to undress.

"Gonna shower then head home… got some things to straighten out."

Overwhelmed by the decision that needed to be made by noon the following day, Gabby paces anxiously from wall to wall of her few-feet-larger-than-tiny dining room. Her phone had been buzzing on her kitchen counter for hours. Unprepared for any topic of conversation, she ignores all calls and text.

"Do you need answers? I can give them to you, just call…"

Gabby is drawn to the television by the old woman inviting all to get answers regarding their future. This makes Gabby giggle and even sits herself down after about an hour of pacing.

You never know how God will speak or who He will speak to you through, Gabby remembers her father's voice as she reaches for the word of God.

"Yep, I certainly need answers…but not from this wannabe Cleo!" Gabby jokes to herself as she opens the bible to the book of Proverbs.

The following morning Gabby felt God had given her what she needed to make the best decision. She prayed that if, for any reason, it is not the right decision to stop it in its tracks. Two weeks later God was still laying tracks for her on this new path.

She removed the content of the manila envelope and signed her name on the dotted line of both the paperwork and check to be cashed.

MOVING AROUND

Preparations for Winston and Arin's wedding had consumed most of Josiah's time allowing Gabby the space she needs to prepare for the move she was soon going to be making.

Gabby decided she needed a change in scenery, inside and out of the office, so she took the job offer Vince presented to her a few months back.

Although he wasn't instantly on team LA, he quickly accepted that this was what Gabby needed for her life right now.

"I was born and raised in the south, Gabby. I happen to love it down here. Though the west coast is not the kind of move I'm looking to make right now, I support your decision to make it," Josiah told her one rainy evening while helping her pack.

When she brought the news to Josiah, she presented it as a choice that had been made, not an option that was up for discussion. He appreciated the way she let him know and respected the fact that she made a decision that was best for her and not based on what he wanted.

"All the women who's independent..." Josiah sang loudly, waving Gabby's scarf in the air.

"That is not how the song goes," she laughs at his attempt to perform.

A few days before Winston and Arin's wedding, Gabby and Josiah take a quick trip to the Midwest to visit the Fawn family.

The trip was his idea but Gabby felt it was perfect. She knew that once she started her new position in LA that she would barely have time to visit.

Josiah was thrilled to meet her mother and the rest of the family. He had spoken with them numerous times via Skype and over the phone but he looked forward to hugs and handshakes from the people who share a bloodline with the woman he loves.

Patrice, Gabby's mother, prepares a large Sunday dinner for the family to serve, despite it being a Friday evening.

It had been years since she had her two daughters under one roof. She was filled with so much joy seeing Gabby and Gina interact and talk about life with each other.

"I can't explain what I feel hearing you two girls laughing together again," Patrice smiles from across the table.

Past achievements, future goals, funny stories and hilarious memories were tossed around throughout the night.

"You two make such a handsome couple. You know Mr. Emmitt, you have a real jewel on your arm there," Gabby's mother winks at him as their visit comes to an end before they leave for the airport.

This brings a smile to Gabby's face and a tear to her eye. That is the exact line her father would say whenever a date came to pick her up and he approved.

She could feel her father's spirit around her. She grabs Josiah's arm tight and inhales, feeling peace in knowing her father was there and he approves.

Gabby shares this with Josiah, and as the plane takes off he asks, "What would your father say if he didn't approve"

Gabby smiles and lays her head on his shoulder.

"Nothing at all."

CHAPTER 8

YES

YES

Hand in hand, Josiah and Gabby walk into the reception hall where Winston and Arin will soon be introduced for the first time as Mr. and Mrs.

Unable to jump into the bustle of being part of the wedding party, Gabby kindly declined Arin's offer to be a bridesmaid just 2 weeks before the wedding. Pleased with her decision, she settles into the mint green linen covered chair reserved for her.

She glances down and smiles at the card that was placed on the table in front of the two seats she and Josiah occupied which read 'Mr. and Mrs. Emmitt'. Gabby wondered who had made the name cards for seat arrangements and assumed it was a member of the bride's family to assume she and Josiah were married.

"Now for the moment you've all been waiting for…well, maybe not you all but I know Gabby has been waiting for this moment, if not all her life, at least for the past six months or so…" Everyone in the room chuckles as the attention turns toward Gabby.

She stares surprised at Winston who was standing in the doorway with his new wife whom, in turn, was smiling from ear to ear as she snatches the microphone from Winston's hand.

"As you all know, I am married now but I always wanted to be a bridesmaid… I am hoping that now I have the opportunity because I would love nothing more than to stand in agreement with you and Josiah when you say your 'I do's'."

Arin, now crying gives the mic back to Winston.

"Well…will you let Arin be a bridesmaid? That is, if you say yes, of course."

Winston nods his head toward Gabby and she turns quickly towards Josiah who was now out of his seat and down on one knee.

Unable to control all the emotions that were now taking over, Gabby gets down on the floor with Josiah, places a kiss on his forehead and accepts his proposal.

The room cheers and the wedding reception resumes with the focus now back on the newlyweds.

The sun was now peeking through the skylights in the high ceilings of the reception hall. This being what they expected, Winston and Arin rented the hall for an entire 24 hours.

Throughout the night the room went from capacity to scarcity but surprisingly about half were still partying at day break.

"Wow, what a night this has been," Josiah says, embracing his, now, fiancé as they dance slowly to no music on an empty dance floor.

He looks at his watch and laughs out loud.

"I don't even want to know," Gabby laughs along knowing it's very early.

BLING BLING

Back in the hotel room, Josiah runs Gabby a warm bubble bath and prepares fruit for her to enjoy while bathing.

"Is this what I get for saying yes?" Gabby jokes as she walks up the steps and then down into the large Jacuzzi tub in the middle of their suite.

Josiah walks over and kneels down alongside the tub.

"I have placed a variety of choices on this platter for you ma'am... please choose what will delight you."

Gabby sits up in the tub so quickly, Josiah is now wet and suds are running down the side of the tub.

"Oh my, they're beautiful." Gabby grabs her face as though her cheeks were about to fall off.

Wiping himself dry he laughs, "I've never seen anyone so excited about strawberries, cantaloupe and raspberries before."

Laughing along, Gabby never takes her eyes off the platter. She is mesmerized by the three rings that were sharing space on the plate with fruit.

"This is not real... this can't be real," she shouts.

"Ok, you got me...one of them is from the crackerjack box but I didn't think you would notice." Josiah jokes.

After several minutes and a few pieces of fruit, Gabby finally makes a decision.

"Did you know I would choose this one," Gabby asks as he slides the two carat princess cut diamond on her finger.

Josiah leans in and kisses Gabby's newly accessorized hand.

"You amaze me every time I am in your presence or hear your voice over the phone; so humble and selfless. Gabby, you have never asked me to do anything but respect you... I love you for that. You knowing who you are has pushed me to find who I am. This is the only way I could properly say thank you for pushing me up a better path without applying pressure."

Both now a blur to one another, words escape them as they fight to see clear through the thick emotion in the room.

Josiah steps into the large tub, clothes and all to embrace his fiancé.

"Ok, this is a bit much," Gabby jokingly complains. "You have officially ruined my bubble bath."

Josiah promises to run her a fresh bath. Pulling him onto her body submerged under the water, she holds him.

"This water is just fine."

MOVING FORWARD

A weekend of festivities made the following week harder to jump into. Monday morning, Gabby was on a flight to Los Angeles, Tuesday morning she was walking into her new place of employment.

Now settled into her new office space, she feels ready to run the new location. It has been a whirlwind making the decision to accept the position, packing up her life in the south and setting up to start a new one on the west coast, but the peace in her spirit let her know she had made the right choice.

Move forward in faith for God has already gone before you to make a way, Gabby can hear her father's voice as she sits and takes in her new surroundings.

After she shared the news of the engagement with her family, they were not very pleased with her decision to take the job and move away. Surprisingly, Gina had two cents to add to all the fuss but it was the shiniest two cent she had ever shared regarding her little sister.

"Go and live the life you want… you can have it all. I wish I had followed my dreams. Didn't know I could do both," Gina advised after a long talk one afternoon.

Gina had opened up to Gabby about Prince. It took a while for Gabby to accept what her sister had done with much prayer. In the end, she knew that forgiveness was the only option. Not only does God's word say so but how could she not forgive when for the last six years that's all she wanted from her sister.

All of Gabby's questions regarding Prince's adoption and what prompted it, Gina answered with no hesitation.

"I only kept it from you because I was angry that I didn't get what I wanted. I didn't tell you about Prince because I didn't think you would care. I pinned you as a child hater or something crazy," Gina admitted.

Gabby let her sister know she was not upset with her and she was happy that she now has a child of her own.

Gina also shared all the horror she experienced during the adoption process. They shared tears and laughs well through the night. Several years of brokenness was repaired in a matter of hours.

Having had some of her past wounds healed, the settling-in process to her new life was easier.

SHE WORKS HARD FOR THE MONEY

"So, how are ya'll gonna plan a wedding and make babies and all that from two different states?" Val calls to voice her concerns to Gabby.

Gabby smiles at the receiver while her friend stridently gives her opinions over her office speaker phone.

"We'll figure that out, you just worry about how you're going to break away from your crazy life to come to Cali and make sure I don't become a complete grandma before I even have children!" The ladies share a laugh.

After the second hour of mindless chatter with Verna, Gabby ends the call with a promise to stay in touch.

She watches out the window from her office as the rain falls over the city. She finds herself missing Josiah's touch. It has been only a week or so since she last held hands and locked eyes with her beloved; a week was more than enough.

Hey, thinking about you...wish you were here

Gabby pats her phone repeatedly on her lap after texting her current thoughts to Josiah.

The phone vibrates in her hand and Josiah's face appears on her screen.

"I didn't say call...hearing your voice now will make it worse," Gabby whines.

She was right; after few moments of speaking with Josiah she is not able to focus, therefore unable to remain in the office.

Retail therapy, she decides, is the only thing to get her through.

Macy's here I come! She thinks to herself as she walks out the glass sliding doors of the eighteen story building and into the rainy Wednesday afternoon.

A new pocket book, two pairs of pumps, three dresses and a quick meal later she is tired and more than ready to get home and rest.

"We really need this and no one has the ability to run this company into the ground like you. Make them give us what we deserve for this broadcast," a colleague says in a call to Gabby.

Gabby immediately regrets answering her cell phone for an unknown number. One of her colleagues felt the need to call and beg for her help. She sighs, now knowing going home to rest is not as close as she wanted.

It took many conversations with many people to agree on a budget that would please her company, as well as theirs. Gabby was delighted with her ability to make everything ok but, displeased with the cost.

She leans all the way back in her comfortable white leather chair and looks up at the ceiling. All the lights are off in her office accept the red and white polka dotted desk lamp gifted to her by the receptionist on the 3rd floor.

"I love your white office but this will make it pop," she smiled a wrinkled sixty-five year old smile.

Gabby spins herself around, sits up and places both hands on her desk. She feels a second wind creeping up her spine and decides she needs to get up before her office becomes her bedroom for the night.

She looks over at the white leather chaise lounge and then quickly over at her closet where she had extra clothes in case of emergencies such as needing to change for a dinner, a meeting or going out for drinks after work.

The morning sun wakes Gabby before her alarm gets the chance. She stretches her hands to the ceiling and yawns big and loud. Feeling rested and glad she came home last night she walks over to her bay window where she smiles out at her neighbor sunbathing in the yard.

"I hope I don't get so LA I think sun bathing in the front yard is cool," she tells Mona, her assistant, who was at her home bright and early to go over the day's demands.

Mona pushes her glasses up to her eyes and smiles. "You are unique and special. I can't see you turning into one of them," she points to the window. Now the sun bathing neighbor has company, two more women lay on the lawn in hopes of a perfect tan.

Gabby observes Mona, admiring her calm and soft, yet edgy personality. You would never know she possessed personality without being around her for a few hours. Her beige wardrobe collection and ponytail give off a complete opposite idea of who she is.

Gabby now noticing the time, showers and dresses to head back to the office.

Months in to her new daily routine, Gabby feels very comfortable and very much accomplished in her new role in the LA office. She has been observing things that appear to her to need change, so she kept notes. With great confidence of all she had gathered she realizes some things need to be ran by Victor, so she has Mona book a Friday night flight back to the south.

SOUTHERN HOSPITALITY

♪*Where my girls at, from the front to the back...*♪ Verna and Tasha sing out loud as they speed down I-85.

Amused and annoyed all at once, Gabby pushes the radio button on the stereo.

"That song is beyond old...how much dust was on that CD when you found it," Gabby grimaced at Verna.

"My girl is in town...can't a broad be happy about that? My happy needs theme music and that was it. Now you get no soundtrack at all," Verna pouts.

Tasha sits forward and rubs Verna's shoulder, "Don't take it personal, she's an LA chick now."

Gabby pulls her dark shades from her pocket book and puts them on, crosses her legs and looks out the passenger window.

"Damn right," she jokes and they all laugh uncontrollably.

Tasha and Verna waste no time going through Gabby's suitcases and claiming things that they knew Gabby wasn't giving up.

"I am supposed to walk around naked this entire week, right," Gabby jokingly snaps as she snatches her clothes from her friends' hands.

The ladies squeeze in lunch and a little shopping before Gabby turns them loose to do their own thing as she had so much to do to prepare for her meeting with Josiah, whom she hoped was made aware of their meeting by now.

Josiah scrolls through his phone while waiting in line for his favorite cup of coffee at Center Coffee Shop.

There were only two people ahead of him but the young lady at the counter seemed to be having a hard time deciding.

"Caramel Macchiato for Josiah" The young lady behind the counter calls out, smiling directly at him as his face was not unfamiliar to her.

"Thank you?" Josiah takes the tall hot drink from her hands and waits for an explanation.

Still wearing a smile the young lady nods toward the back of the coffee shop where, on the table, sat a red gift bag with white, red and yellow tissue paper sprouting from it.

Josiah looks back and forth between her and the gift bag a few times before walking over. Leaning against the bag was a card that read his name on the envelope.

Many are the miles I would fly, drive or even walk to get to you...Gabby

He puts the card down on the table and takes another look up at the young lady behind the counter who was still smiling, but, now joined by two other employees of Center Coffee Shop.

Pulling the tissue paper from the bag slowly, Josiah eventually pulls up a hotel room key with it. There was a sticky note with the room number and a time.

Josiah gathers his surprise and begins to leave. Just before exiting, he turns to thank the young lady for assisting Gabby.

He looks at his watch and makes a mental note that he has eight hours before it's time to show up at the Westin.

GETTING READY

Gabby spends almost an entire day in Frederick's of Hollywood looking for the perfect *take me now* outfit to wear for Josiah tonight. She anticipated bringing Val along but, because she wanted something she could be cute and comfortable in, she knew Val would be of no help. Val had no sense of comfort when it came to anything sexual. After going through rack by rack of lingerie more than once, Gabby finally decides on the set that she believes is best for the night. She brings it along with massaging oil, sex dice and handcuffs to the register.

The blushing smile she wore when approaching the register quickly fades once the cashier opens his mouth.

"Oh, someone's looking for a good time tonight." The young man at the register was clearly the opposite of heterosexual and flaunted every bit of his lifestyle choice.

Gabby smiles an annoyed smile and quickly speaks up, "Mind your business and do your job, kid."

A few more stops in the mall, then Gabby heads to the hotel room to set up for the evening.

"Hi, this is Gabby Fawn, the one who brought the gift bag and purchased the coffee. Did he show?"

Now confirmed that her plan is unfolding perfectly she begins to get excited, causing her nerves to kick in overtime.

Seven o'clock rolls around and she can hardly contain her excitement. Switching positions at least ten times, Gabby became frustrated. She couldn't decide which was the sexiest way to position herself on the large love seat which sat in front of a large picture window overlooking the city.

She fumbles a little more before glancing over at the wall clock once more, a quarter to, and she still had no clue what her sexy pose was going to be.

Suddenly she hears the lock open at the door of her suite and before she knew it she was on her feet. *"So much for sitting sexy,"* she whispers to herself as she places her hands gently on her hips and bends slightly to the left while crossing her legs, right in front of left.

She quickly whips a smile on her face and wonders if she looks as stiff and uncomfortable as she feels.

The look on Josiah's face once he enters the room says she mastered sexy in that moment.

CHAPTER 9

CHANGES

AT THE CENTER OF IT ALL…A LOVE STORY

CHANGES

"So, while we were apart I had a lot of time to think." Josiah reaches across the table and grabs Gabby's hand to hold in his own.

Gabby sits up in her chair letting him know her attention is all his.

"I let Claude know that I need a break from the company. I have been advising people on their finances for too long, I don't believe that's what I am supposed to die doing."

Attentively listening, Gabby just stares into Josiah's eyes. She didn't want to interrupt any thoughts that were currently in his head.

He needs to vent, and I am going to let him, despite this lace irritating the crack of my behind, Gabby thinks to herself.

Josiah continues on for quite a while and not once did Gabby chime in. Eye and hand contact was lost somewhere between "It's been a great learning experience" and "I can't believe the time I've wasted".

Josiah finally reaches a point of silence. Gabby takes over word duty…with caution.

"I support you in anything you decide to do," she assures him. "You are absolutely amazing in every way… respectful, patient, gentle, kind…I could go on and on about all the great things you are but the one that you need to really be reminded of in this moment is you are smart and you can do whatever you put your mind to."

Josiah stares into the smiling face of the woman he loves. Though her words were simple, they were perfect and what he needed to hear.

"I love you," is all he could get past his lips without, in his mind, making a fool of himself.

Josiah stands up and takes a couple steps away from the dining table where he and Gabby had been talking since he walked through the door of the hotel room.

Neglecting to vocally tell Gabby what his face had clearly spoke when he had seen her standing half naked in front of the window, he immediately asked her to sit and talk with him.

Though he was very much turned on by her appearance he had to clear his mind first.

Mind now cleared, he gestures for her to follow him to the bedroom. He and Gabby have had some close calls when it came to sex but they always found a way past the temptation.

Tonight was different and she didn't find a subtle way to tell him that she has no desire to fight temptation tonight.

When they reach the bedroom Josiah sits on the bed and stares at Gabby before him in a baby blue and silver lace with ribbon corset which matched the thong that rested perfectly on her full hips.

He spins her around and admires the ribbon tied in a bow right at the small of her back just before the rest of the thong went into hiding.

He bends down to remove her silver high-heel pumps one at a time and kisses up from leg to each thigh going back and forth as if to see which is sweeter to his lips.

"Untie your corset," Josiah instructs as he slides back onto the king size bed to watch.

With no words, Gabby does as he requests. Although nervous, she constantly reminds herself to stay in character.

"Let those thongs drop."

Gabby fumbles and begins to lose character. She glances down at the beautiful engagement ring Josiah had placed on her finger weeks ago.

You're fine girl. He put a ring on it, she reminds herself as she slowly slips the underwear to the ground. She is suddenly feeling sexier than ever. She holds her head up and stands tall with her shoulders back while displaying a sexy smirk on her face.

Josiah slides to the edge of the bed and grabs Gabby by her waist. He begins to kiss her from neck to shoulder, chest to stomach, on down to where her juices are surely flowing.

He drops to his knees and presses his forehead into her stomach and holds her for a while before finally lifting her to the bed.

ANOTHER AGAIN

Morning comes and Josiah has made a decision regarding his future...or so he thinks.

"I will sell my place, move with pops and take care of him."

Gabby rolls over in the bed and stares at Josiah for a moment. A lot tired and a little irritated that he was still on the topic; she was hoping his eyes were closed and that he was talking in his sleep.

"Babe, your mother and father are back together whether you like it or not. He has the person he needs to take care of him."

Though her intention was not to be negative, it didn't quite fall positive on his ears. Josiah turns away from her and she knows that the little boy inside of him is about to surface.

He has spent more time than ever with his mother lately and has even said he's forgiven her in his heart but, it is still a sticky subject.

Gabby rubs Josiah's back, "Maybe they both can use your assistance."

Josiah scoots closer to the edge of the bed out of Gabby's reach.

"Who took care of me when I was growing up," he reminds Gabby, as well as himself, of the pain he felt as a little boy.

A little frustrated, Gabby sits up in the bed and scoots herself over to Josiah wrapping her legs around him from behind. Cheek to back she holds him tight.

"What you are feeling is real and you have every right to feel however you want about the harm that was done to you as a child. As a man, you can choose how those feelings affect your life. Harboring feelings of pain and resentment only hurts you. Do you like being in pain?"

Another attempt at positive speaking goes wrong. Josiah receives her words and makes a choice, choosing to be angry.

"As a man, I am telling you this conversation is over. You as a woman have the right to feel however you want to about that."

Gabby sits on the edge of the bed and watches as Josiah gathers his clothes from the floor. He slips on his pants but doesn't bother putting on anything else.

He reaches into his pocket and pulls out the room key which he tosses onto the nightstand.

"I am sure you won't be in town too much longer, have a safe flight back to LA."

THE BLAME GAME

"I told you, you should have chosen the pink one trimmed with red lace," Verna attempts to humor Gabby while riding through downtown on a horse and carriage.

Business was handled earlier that afternoon with Victor at the old office building. She was greeted pleasantly by all who knew her and given the side eye by those who didn't.

After all, she strutted through the main doors in her all-white pencil skirt suit with salmon colored accessories and taupe Steve Madden pumps. Her thick natural curls seemed to be flowing as though a diva fan was pointed in her direction.

"I am not sure what I wore even mattered. He is dealing with some issues that I need to realize I can't fix. How can I support something he is not even sure he wants to do, you know," Gabby asks while holding the side of the carriage for dear life as though going 55 mph.

Gabby glares over at Verna who had stopped listening earlier on in the conversation than Gabby had expected. She was posing and taking multiple selfies to send her newest fling.

Rain was falling when Gabby left LA and it greeted her coming back.

Three days in Atlanta had been more than enough but having left with unanswered questions makes it a little harder to go about business as usual.

"Scattered showers for the remainder of the day, keep your umbrellas close and your rain boots closer. It will be coming down all week."

Turning off the television within seconds of turning it on, Gabby curls up in the corner of her tan leather sectional and prays herself to sleep.

Vibration disturbs her slumber. The screen on her phone, the only light in the room, was almost blinding seeing that all she had been looking at was the back of her eyelids for the past four hours.

Her mother's face soon disappeared from the screen leaving the notification that her call was missed.

"Why does he call her before me," Gabby questions knowing the answer.

After the proposal and the trip Midwest to visit her family, Josiah has been making it a point to contact Patrice, Gabby's mother, regarding just about everything that went on between them. Granted he didn't discriminate and filled her in on both good and bad. It was still a bit much for Gabby to take.

Surprised she had stayed asleep so long on the sofa, she decides to just stay there for the night. She removes her flying attire; leggings, blazer and bra, tossing them on the chair on the other side of the coffee table and settles back into comfort on the couch.

I APOLOGIZE

A pounding at the door startles Gabby out of her sleep. Grabbing her phone to check the time, she becomes even more startled. The pounding at the door gets louder as Gabby races to clothe her body before heading to the door to go completely off on whoever was on the other side of it.

"Wait a minute," she yells from the middle of her walk in closet where she is pulling a jersey style t-shirt that reads *who run this...* in bold red letters on the front and *Ladies* in bold red letters across the back over her head.

This shirt was worn by her and Tasha in college every Saturday afternoon in the fall when the female dorm hall went up against the male dorm hall in a game of flag football. The men's shirts were not half as exciting; they simply read Roaring Lions across the back. The ladies often brought them down to a meow by the end of most games.

The pounding continues. Fully dressed and baseball bat in hand, Gabby is ready to face the person of rage outside her home.

"As, usual you were right. I am man enough to admit that. Still no excuse though, I need to get my shi..."

Josiah pauses and turns to face Gabby who was still standing at the opened door with the baseball bat in her hands ready to swing.

"Watch your mouth in this house." Gabby tosses the wooden bat onto the waxed wooden floor and moves quickly towards Josiah.

Leaping into his arms, Josiah braces himself to catch her. There was so much heat forming between them that the front of their clothes became damp almost instantly... and that wasn't the only thing on Gabby.

Josiah had too much on his mind that he needed to vent off to Gabby back in Georgia at the hotel. He arrived with the intention to sit and catch up, not lay up. He made a decision that night that he was going to stick to what he knew she truly wanted.

"Engaged doesn't mean married, Gabby. When we met you told me you were holding out for marriage and I decided from that moment...well, maybe not right at that moment, but when I accepted you I accepted your wishes. I am going to marry you, it just hasn't happened yet, therefore this won't either."

He told her while holding her nude body in his trembling arms that night. In that moment she wanted him more than when she first planned it all out in her head but at the same time she loved and respected him more also.

"What are you doing?"

Josiah grabs Gabby by the waist and lowers her off of him.

"I thought you were going to be upset or--"

"Or what?" Gabby interrupts.

Josiah seats himself and looks up at Gabby now towering over him.

"...or pissed, or hurt or furious," she continues.

Feeling like there was nothing else to do or say, Josiah apologizes.

"You know, that's the thing about love Josiah...it gets complicated and it even hurts sometimes. But the beauty of the ugly shows up when it's time to resolve...and we resolve every time."

Josiah reaches for Gabby's hands, but she moves them to her head as though to display she is thinking of what to say next, so they land on her thighs. He begins to squeeze them gently as she goes on.

"I decided to accept your wishes when I accepted you as well."

"What wishes were those? You were the only one that came in with demands," Josiah chuckles.

"To let you be who you are and support what makes you happy and push you toward what you feel you can't reach."

Gabby walks away from his grip and begins pacing back and forth.

"You're so stubborn and you anger at the first word you don't like out of someone else's mouth. So, I will be your gentleness, calming the anger that arises whether my fault or not. You love to be there for your father because he was there for you. So I will help in whatever way I can and not judge your decisions regarding him…"

Gabby wipes her forehead as though running a marathon causing her to sweat profusely as she continues.

"There is nothing that you don't believe you can reach, I agree. But just in case you forget, babe, I will be your reminder…your stair step…ladder, whatever you need to reach whatever it is."

As the tears make their way down Gabby's face, Josiah sits still trying to keep his from falling.

They stare into each other's eyes for what seemed like a lifetime.

A WHOLE NEW WORLD

"Hope you like pancakes made with oats. Not the Aunt Jemima's mix."

Gabby stands at the breakfast bar picking sleep out the corners of her eyes while Josiah searches from cabinet to cabinet for what he needs to prepare a healthy breakfast.

"Oats?"

Josiah laughs at the disgusted look on Gabby's face. He walks over and kisses her on the forehead, then pulls a stool from beneath the bar.

"Have a seat, my lady. You will enjoy it. Oh yeah, a young lady came to the door, said she was your assistant but I told her you weren't working today."

Quickly jumping up from the stool, Gabby begins to look frantically for her cell phone.

"Josiah, you should have woken me up."

Gabby soon made her way to the office. Though she was frazzled for arriving in the middle of the afternoon, the worry was not significant. One of the perks of her role is that she creates her own schedule.

True to who she is though, her dedication to what she put her time into overpowered the leverage she had in her position.

"...last, but not least, we still need to reach out to Charleston to see where they are with their upcoming projects."

Mona diligently takes notes as Gabby walks in circles while in vocal thought.

"Ms. Fawn, I am so sorry for showing up at your house this morning. It's just that I do every morning and, I must admit, I didn't check my emails before arrival so if you emailed to tell me not..."

"Mona..." Gabby cuts Mona's plea for forgiveness short.

"We are here now and you are doing your job. If there are any issues that need to be addressed regarding your responsibilities, I will address them accordingly."

Mona pushes her glasses to her face and lowers her head as though she had been reprimanded. Gabby notices and instantly feels bad.

"Let's grab a coffee," Gabby suggests hoping to lighten the mood.

Once Gabby and Mona got past the first twenty minutes of awkward silence, the conversation began to flow, thanks to the lady who came in fully dressed in sweats and boots as though it wasn't uncomfortably hot outside.

"Looking at her is making me sweat," they agreed and the conversation went on from there.

DISCONNECTED

"How was your day?" Josiah closes his laptop and walks over to greet Gabby at the door with a kiss and to relieve her of the briefcase and grocery bags in her hands.

She gladly hands them over and continues to walk by dismissing his attempt to converse about her day.

Now accustomed to her mood changes, he decides to allow her space and goes back to work accepting a call on his business line.

In the bedroom, Gabby changes into something more comfortable as she tries to come up with the best way to talk with Josiah about his loss of purpose and her new sense of.

Uncomfortable with the negative space she knows she created when she walked in the door she anxiously steps into the living room to resolve whatever was unresolved from her trip to Georgia and what happened this morning with him dismissing Mona.

"Set the appointment for the following week. I should be back in town then but I'll need time to review their file. It's been a good three years since they've needed our counsel."

Glad to hear Josiah talking business… his business… Gabby's mood makes a drastic shift.

He's come to his senses, she thought as she happily skips over to him on the sofa.

Just as her mood had shifted, so has his. She picks up on it after he shifts his body away from her on the sofa while wrapping up his conversation.

"Sure thing, Claude. Will check in with you once I'm back on southern soil."

"How's Claude? You should have told him hello for me."

"He's well." Josiah tosses his phone onto the cluttered table.

The television was on the smooth grooves music station and the soft voice of Sade was filling the room.

Josiah goes into the kitchen to take the lasagna he made from scratch out of the oven.

Gabby's attempts to soften the tension to match the mood Sade's voice was giving off were unsuccessful. Every question she asked was answered in one word or less, with less being a smirk.

"I have tomorrow off... let's plan the day," Gabby exclaims in a last attempt to perk Josiah up.

"Guess you like French dressing because that's all you have in here. Salad is tossed and in the white bowl on the second shelf," he informs her while his head is still in the fridge.

"Where can I go running around here...like a park or trail close by?" No eye contact made, Josiah ignores the fact that Gabby is now standing right in front of him.

"Running? You've been here all day. Why run now that I'm home?"

Ignoring her question just as she had his, he lets her know dinner is ready just before exiting the kitchen to change into running gear.

SHELTER

An hour into flipping through channels on the television there's a knock at Gabby's door. Assuming she already knows who's on the other side she swings it open. But to her surprise Josiah was not on the other side.

"It's after ten, what are you doing here?"

Gabby grabs her unannounced guest by the arm into the foyer. Just before closing the door she notices a duffel bag on the step.

"What is this about?"

Her guest begins sobbing uncontrollably.

"Wow, company tonight, Gabby?" Josiah pushes his way in the door, out of breath and clearly in the same mood he was in before he left to run.

"Is this the best time for a sleepover," he hints at the bag blocking the doorway.

"Josiah, Mona; Mona, Josiah... my fiancé."

"Fiancé?" Mona begins to gather herself and head toward the door.

"I had no idea, I am so sorry to have bothered you. I'll see you bright and early Monday morning. You are off tomorrow."

Shocked and confused Gabby, is at a loss for words. She watches as Mona makes her way out the front door and down the stairs.

"What was that about," Josiah asks, not knowing she knows as much as he does...nothing.

"Not sure, she just showed up. You should shower before dinner. I've already eaten."

While Josiah showers Gabby sits and talks through some things with him. Although unresponsive, she knows he would have no choice but to listen closely to her while in the shower. She knew his mind was always clear there.

"This is new for me and I understand it is new for you as well. In the beginning of our relationship, my time was freer, my presence was obviously more available and I didn't have anyone working for me. It took some getting used to for me and my selfish self didn't realize you would need time to adjust as well."

By the time his dinner was heated and placed in front of him, Josiah had forgiven Gabby for her side of the disagreement and also apologized for his. They found a happy median agreeing that they are both going through life transformations and that both need to respect change, even if they don't fully understand it.

"Did you ever find out what was going on with...I think you said her name was Mona?"

Gabby jumps up from the bed to grab her cell phone and call to check on Mona. Though she hesitates once she sees the time on her phone reads well after midnight, she still calls knowing she won't sleep without knowing the girl is alright.

The phone begins to ring… in her ear and surprisingly outside her window as well.

"You hear that?" Josiah walks over to the window that was cracked open so they could enjoy the California fall night breeze.

Instead of going to the window, Gabby goes out the front door and walks around the house to find Mona laying there on a thin sheet, using her duffel bag for a pillow.

Mona sits up, startled as Gabby approaches. "I usually power it off at night…we aren't even allowed to have cell phones in the shelter." Mona turns the volume down on her phone and lays back down on her duffel bag.

CHAPTER 10

EVERYTHING HAPPENS FOR A REASON

EVERYTHING HAPPENS FOR A REASON

After a late afternoon lunch at the small privately owned deli a couple blocks from home, Gabby decides to take a much needed walk through the large, but often, vacant park nearby.

"I don't want to come down. I can see better from up here anyway!"

A small voice shouts from high in the branches of a very large tree near the middle of the park.

Gabby walks slowly toward the tree and watches anxiously as a young man, both feet firmly on the ground tries to talk the child down.

"Ok, I am sorry for whatever it is you probably think I did." The young man sounds more annoyed than afraid and this concerns Gabby causing her motherly instinct to kick in.

"Usually to help people we have to meet them where they are...afraid of heights," Gabby asks the young man, interjecting herself into the matter.

The man gives Gabby the once over and turns back to continue shouting what she thinks is non-sense at the boy.

"Kid, I will call your mom to get you. I want her to come just as bad as you do."

Gabby steps in front of the man, studying the tree to figure out the best way to climb up to the child. When she reaches the branch where the child is sitting, she positions herself in the fold of another branch extended from the tree. Looking at the child, her heart breaks. She could sense the fear...not of heights but of something else.

"When I was a little girl, I would climb the tree in my neighbor's yard when they weren't home. From the height of that tree I could see the main

139

highway that connected east to west and I would watch and wait for my father to get home from work."

The child remains silent but a smile appears.

"Awww, now that's different. When I would be sitting in the tree there was no way I would wear a smile. No, I was sad...alone and confused. Bet you don't know anything about those feelings...do you?"

The smile on the child's face opens up and laughter pours into the cool air.

"Girls don't climb trees!"

Gabby joins the child in laughter while trying to wipe away the look on her face that she was sure gave her confusion away.

The child had blonde hair that was so long it hung over the branch they were sitting on, wearing a purple jacket, jeans and tan and purple boots. Gabby was certain she was in the company of a little girl.

"My name is Gabby...what's yours?" She extends her hand.

Laughter stops and the child goes back to a silent frown.

"Hey, what are you saying to my kid?"

Grateful that the man down below couldn't see her face, she didn't try to cover up the confusion that swept over it once again. The man looks to be no older than twenty, and that was pushing it.

"My mom takes a long time to get back when she drops me here. I wish I was back in Arizona but we couldn't stay there."

Though Gabby is glad the child is speaking up, she is still anxious for a name...better yet a gender.

"How long is long," she asks while searching the child with her eyes.

"Time to come down, now, Kyle and don't listen to anything that stranger is saying to you.

"Your father is right. I am a stranger but I want to help you, if that's ok?"

The boy stands between branches, revealing to be taller than he seemed while sitting and begins to climb down.

"You can't help me; my parents have already been picked."

She watches as the father angrily grabs hold of the boy and shakes him while rambling off all the reasons why he's upset.

HIDDEN PAIN

Now out of the tree, home and showered Gabby paces the floor feeling unsuccessful in her efforts to help the boy.

"It's like he didn't care about the kid. He was just mad because the kid was interrupting the flow of his day! Crazy, right?" Gabby rants to Josiah via Skype. She decides on a visual call because she wants to show the scars she collected from tree climbing.

"The moral of the story is what," Josiah asks with a smirk on his face.

Already knowing what he's thinking, she slams the laptop closed, ending their call.

It has been just over a week since Josiah left and Mona took his place in the house. Gabby couldn't find it in her heart to allow Mona to go back to a shelter. More selfishly, she wanted to keep her around to find out just how life got like this for such a young, but smart, girl.

Needing to get her mind off the boy in the tree and onto something else, Gabby decides to go through her old things to find new things for Mona.

Dress up is always fun! she thinks to herself as she heads to the garage.

Well over an hour passes and Gabby soon grows tired from searching through the many totes she dragged in.

Sitting and looking over all the clothes she pulled out, she begins feeling guilty about not ever giving them to either of her longtime friends who had been begging for her things for years.

As she pulled pieces from the totes she could hear Verna's voice in her head, *"oh, it's like that…thought we was better than that! You know I been wanting that since you bought it…"*

Gabby is by no means a Carrie Bradshaw of fashion or even a Samantha Jones, for that matter. She was more of a Charlotte in style: no matter what she wore, it was always a nice fresh look. The look many women try to achieve but, when shopping for it, never really know where to start.

"It's really no big deal; I have enough…" Mona expresses in the most sincere tone as she walks into the room and is greeted by piles of clothes and emptied totes.

Gabby had sent her a text letting her know about her task for the day.

Annoyed, she throws her hand up in Mona's face.

"You have been here a week and I am tired of those two skirts you keep wearing. Aren't you?" As soon as the words left her mouth, she regretted saying them.

Mona sits and sinks down into the chair across from Gabby, hesitant to respond, at first. Not because she doesn't know what to say but because her answer is the opposite of how Gabby feels. What her boss doesn't know is the few things she did have, including the skirts, held sentimental value to her.

"No, I am not tired of them…don't think I ever will be," Mona finally speaks up. "When my Nana's house burned down, the things in this bag is all that I was able to grab. To my surprise, all but the three skirts belonged to me…the skirts, to my mother who died when I was about ten. I knew my Nana had her clothing put away. I don't even remember where I was when I grabbed the stuff I have…flames were everywhere."

Mona drops her head and tears begin to fall from her eyes onto the red and beige pencil skirt Gabby has expressed a lack of like for.

"Gabby, I have no one left. My Grandma's bible and my mother's skirts are all I have of my family."

142

Mona's fair skin was quickly turning red as she gasps through the pain of remembering what she has recently experienced.

Gabby maneuvers through the totes to get to Mona and embrace her. She comforts her just as she imagined her mother or grandmother would have if they were there.

"I had no right to judge you like that, and I sincerely apologize."

Gabby loosens her embrace enough to lean back and look Mona in the eye.

"If you'll let me, I will be what you don't have but desperately need...family. I would also like to be your friend. This stuff... all materialistic. Thanks for putting me back in my place."

Mona smiles at Gabby and then breaks out into a laugh, "Yeah, it is materialistic but I still want that stuff."

They laugh together as they continue sorting through Gabby's totes of fashion's past together.

YOU WERE RIGHT

Fighting past the embarrassment of admitting she was wrong, Gabby places a much needed call to Josiah.

"Again I ask..."

Gabby smiles. Josiah's tone lets her know he is not angry with her.

"The moral of the story is...I need to mind my own business,." she finishes his sentence.

Laughter takes over the conversation for a brief moment.

Gabby shares with Josiah her blind eye to Mona and her situation and how she allowed herself to yet again butt in where she should leave well enough alone.

In all the time that has passed, Josiah knew Gabby enough to know her intentions are never malicious.

"Wish I was there to kiss your forehead and tell you it's ok."

Gabby feels her heart melting. She loved how every time she admitted a flaw to Josiah he just wanted to make sure she was okay.

"Well, my independent, nosey and beautiful lady, I must go now. Time difference, you know?"

"Good night and I love you brought the conversation to a close."

Gabby decides to make a list of all the times she could recall butting into someone else's business trying to help, but it all went wrong. By the time she gets to the 3rd sheet of notebook paper, she realizes she has a major problem.

She looks over at the nightstand where her bible was resting and immediately feels guilty. She hasn't really read it like she use to in Georgia.

Sitting knees to chest in her king sized bed, she rests her head on her knees and exhales deeply.

"Changes need to be made," she admits aloud as she slowly drifts into dream land.

The smell of bacon pulls Gabby from her bed and into the kitchen where Mona was preparing breakfast the following morning. She looks at the table and notices there were place settings for three.

"Good morning! Breakfast is almost ready!"

She joins Mona in the kitchen to retrieve the orange juice from the refrigerator.

"Mona, I never apologized for what I did yesterday. I should have asked you if you wanted my stuff and never should have assumed."

Briefly looking up from the eggs she is scrambling, Mona smiles at Gabby and nods toward the table.

"Have a seat. I'll pour that into a glass for you." Mona pulls down two glasses from the cabinet and meets Gabby at the table.

"Are we waiting on a 3rd guest," she asks, looking again at the extra place setting.

Mona begins filling their plates with bacon, cheesy eggs, grits and biscuits… but only two of the three plates.

"When I would have a misunderstanding with my Nana, mother…or anyone in the family, the meal that followed the confrontation would be when we set an extra place for whatever we were carrying. I would have to fill it up with all that is not healthy for me as I took in nutrients that were."

Still confused, Gabby's eyes shift from Mona to the empty chair.

"So, is a mediator coming? I didn't think it was that serious."

Mona laughs, "We are our own mediator, or at least should be in most situations. When you truly care about someone it doesn't take an outsider to make you realize your wrongs toward another. Not that you were wrong to me and I certainly hope I am not being wrong toward you…just thought this would be good for you to try."

STAY OR GO

On the road headed home from visiting with his father and uncle, Josiah decides to exit the highway and do some window shopping.

"Yeah man, the weather is a lot different over in LA. I need a whole new wardrobe." Josiah and Winston have been having phone conversations every day, at least twice a day, since the wedding.

"So, you're really going to make this move, huh, bro," Winston, unable to hide his uncertainty asks. "I mean, without even telling her?"

Josiah laughs at his brothers concern.

"What do you think about capris for men? Cool or nah?" Josiah averts conflict by ignoring already answered questions.

"Nah…that's not even cool in LA, bro." They laugh together.

A few minutes of window shopping turned into a few hours of in store shopping. Two suits, three ties and a pair of loafers later Josiah realizes he is late to a very important meeting.

Though this marks the first time of seven years in business for himself he is late, he just knew Claude was anxiously awaiting his arrival to the office to rub it in his face.

To his surprise, when he arrived at the office, there were balloons and banners invading the office space but no one there that he could see.

"SURPRISE!"

Winston, Arin, Claude and many of the people they do business with appeared from under desks and behind closed doors.

Claude steps before the crowd holding up a sign, *Moving on up like George and Weezy!*

Josiah embraces his business partner while laughing out loud.

"What is all this about?"

"That's what I want to know, you're never late," Claude reminds him.

A couple of hours into celebrating, they realize the spirits are running low which prompts them to take the party to a nearby tavern.

"Gabby is going to be surprised to see you stepping up and making this move. You're a great man for this. It's often the woman that has to up-root her life for the man," Arin boosts Josiah.

As the group mingles and chats amongst themselves, Josiah finds himself withdrawing from the moment into a mental space of doubt and confusion.

Taking time to really think this decision through was never really an option. The way he sees it, the woman he loves is following her heart and wherever she is, that's where he wants to be. Simple enough, he thought.

After their rollercoaster conversation regarding his indecisiveness with life and where he should be, he realized that Gabby was right. Being a grown man, he must move forward with life and what makes him happy. Granted he loves his father very much but some of the time spent was to get back at his mom.

Although it was hard for him to understand how his father could love a woman that has repeatedly shattered his heart, he wanted to have that kind of dedication and love for one woman for the rest of his life... Gabby.

Winston recognizes the look on his brother's face but decides to leave him to answer the questions brewing on his own.

"I know this is the right choice. I Love Gab, you know...you'd do it for Arin wouldn't you," Josiah asks Winston, calling later in the night to see if his plan to leave him to his own questions worked in his favor.

Winston laughs, "Hey, only one of us can be totally, crazy in love."

GEORGIA

Phone tag was the game of the day for Josiah and Gabby. Both placing unsuccessful calls and eventually growing tired of the chase leaves their communication up to fate. Both had the same intent to inform the other of big news but for some reason the universe was against either having knowledge of it.

The unknowing didn't mean undoing though. Flights have been booked, homes rented, jobs accepted and belongings packed and shipped.

Calls to Gabby were unsuccessful, but many calls to and from the law firm in Los Angeles were taken while Josiah was trying to gather himself for the ride to the airport.

"You are going to love Georgia. It is a beautiful and inexpensive place to live. So much to do, so many people..." Gabby takes Mona by the hand and searches her eyes for excitement, but there was none.

"I know this is a huge step to take but you are twenty-two years old and your entire life is ahead of you. The life you had here is no more…why not build a new foundation to grow on?"

Gabby, searching Mona's eyes is disappointed yet again, there's nothing there.

"Ms. Fawn, that about does it," one of the four movers Gabby hired informs her.

She glances out the window at the large truck that was loaded and locked.

"Wow, that was quick," Gabby exhales while writing out the advance payment check required to get her things on the road back south.

"Why the hell would you let them *out of this country* people move your stuff in a truck through states. That is crazy girl!" Verna's voice carries from the cell phone through the empty bathroom in the airport.

"Those 'out of this country' people got an *A* from the Better Business Bureau. I am sure my things are fine. Just worry about being at the airport on time, chick."

Gabby leans against the wall outside the bathroom and watches Mona as she cries what Gabby hopes will be her last tears of sadness.

"Let her know that she is welcome to join you but let her make the final decision," Gabby's mother told her during their weekly phone conversation earlier that week. Gabby's family was well aware of her decision to move back to Georgia. She had to constantly remind her mom not to share the news with Josiah, seeing that they have a somewhat close relationship now.

"I can hold water. That's why so many people dump theirs on me," her mother promptly told her.

Unlike the preparation for the move, the flight was very smooth except for shortly after boarding. Many of the passengers grew frustrated because there was a slight delay due to a plane stranded on the runway. Of course, when you're anxious to get somewhere, five minutes feels like five hours.

Mona remains in deep sleep the entire way while Gabby enjoys oldie but goodies music and reads an assortment of magazines provided by the flight attendant in first class. The attendant aggressively offers beverages of the adult kind a number of times as well, but she refuses every time. Assuming she could see that her nerves were getting the best of her Gabby made a minor deal of it.

"Fly with us again soon," The attendant says, smiling as Gabby and Mona exit the aircraft. They feel the chill of the fall air and shudder briefly.

"I can already tell we are no longer in LA." Mona whispers to herself while looking at the people rushing through the airport. Gabby pats her back, "This is only the beginning."

CHAPTER 11

AT THE CENTER OF IT ALL

AT THE CENTER OF IT ALL…A LOVE STORY

AT THE CENTER OF IT ALL

The bustle of the crowd doesn't slow Josiah down one bit. Being that he was always on time for everything in life, a flight to Los Angeles would be no different, or so he thought. Looking down at his watch while pushing through the crowd he realizes he is truly pressed for time.

Traffic on the way to the airport was minimal. The delay was due to Arin making a few wrong turns before finally getting on the highway.

Smooth Jazz filled the new Toyota Camry gifted to Arin, by Winston, the night of their wedding. It was like an episode of My Sweet 16 on MTV.

"Everyone step out to the front of the building for me please," Winston announced to all the guests.

To everyone's surprise, and most importantly Arin's, there it was wrapped in a big red ribbon: the latest model Camry, white with camel leather interior and all the bells and whistles. Arin had been driving a 1994 Buick since her junior year in high school. Although she loved the old Buick very much, and it never really gave her any issues, Winston made it clear that once she became Mrs. Saud, she would no longer be driving that car.

"What if she is upset that you didn't speak with her about this life changing event? You know how Gabby gets," Winston cuts through the calm of the smooth Jazz a little more than halfway to their destination.

Annoyed that Winston decided to share the backseat with him while his carry-on occupied the front where Arin was driving, Josiah gives him the look that he hoped would stop the "what ifs".

Still concerned, Winston tries to get Josiah to see different ways this can play out. Even though Josiah uttered not one word, Winston kept it up all the way there.

Convinced he is making the right choice Josiah, has learned to tune every other thought and opinion out that has been coming his way since he announced his decision.

Finally reaching the gate, Josiah stops a moment to catch his breath. *This was way more intense than my morning runs,* he thinks to himself as he approaches the attendant behind the desk.

"Where is everyone?"

The flight attendant points to the screen above her head, "This flight departed ten minutes ago, sir."

Josiah sits in one of the many empty chairs at gate F11 and throws his head down into his hands.

"Would you like for me to check for later flight times to Los Angeles, sir?"

BACK

Keys in hand, Gabby walks up to the door of her new townhome in a brand new development. It stood near the city and had a reasonable walking distance to work. The building had all the amenities she wanted and more. She is even able to make it her own in just about any way she feels necessary outside of tearing down and rebuilding despite the fact that it is a rental property.

"There are four rooms in here. You are welcome to pick whichever one will suit you best, except the master of course," Gabby nudges Mona who still appears to be a little shocked.

Mona gasps once Gabby opens the door. The room, which was all hers, was bigger than she was used to.

"So, I have never really had a roommate. Just my Grandma and mom. Oh, and occasionally whoever was in the shelter the same night I was."

Gabby sees fear in Mona's eyes and gets concerned.

"We can run up to the bookstore and grab *How to be a Roommate for Dummies.* I hear it's very helpful."

Mona looks over at her momentarily, uncertain of her sincerity. Although she knows it isn't a real book, she will never admit to Gabby, or anyone else, that she wishes it was.

"Yes, a right and two lefts you can't miss it," Gabby fusses on the phone with the delivery man from the furniture store. She had ordered Mona's bedroom furniture three days ago which should have arrived an hour ago.

"Great choice! The view is almost as good as mine," Gabby says, standing next to Mona in her chosen room. It was one of two on the upper level. Although almost identical in size, the one Gabby chose was on the right side of the house which provided great views of the Atlanta city skyline.

"I know you're right below me...if that will be a problem I can take the other room."

Gabby laughs as she walks over the window, "Don't be silly. You made an excellent choice...and just in time, the movers have finally arrived."

SET BACK

"The signs...read them man! They are all over the place." Winston's ranting seems to have continued even after Josiah exited the car a half hour ago because he was still at it when Josiah, unfortunately, had to get back in.

"Come on man, now is really not the time," Josiah informs him, tired, emotional and a little stressed. He dials the number to the only voice that is able to soothe him these days. Yet still, phone tag is in effect.

Baby, haven't heard your voice all day...I kind of need to. Call me?

Just before pressing the end button on the screen, a new call is coming through from a California number.

Winston watches closely and grows concerned as he watches his brothers face drop. He couldn't get much from the conversation as all Josiah's responses consisted of "yes...ok...I see." The conversation finally ended with, "I appreciate your time. Keep in touch."

Once again, knowing his brother, Winston keeps all the questions bubbling in his mind to himself. He faces the front and places his hand on his wife's leg as he watches the road ahead.

"Looks can be deceiving," Arin says, placing a cup of hot tea on the dining room table in front of Josiah before joining Winston at the window. "There was no sign of rain, but it's falling."

Josiah lifts his head briefly to see the drops of rain on the glass before lowering it back down, all the way down on the table, this time.

Hours gone, Josiah finds himself in the same spot and the tea Arin made untouched and, now, cold. The rain has eased up but the storm is still very severe within Josiah.

"Your phone has been buzzing in your jacket pocket, but you seemed in such deep thought. I didn't want to interrupt."

Arin hands her brother-in-law his jacket.

Three missed calls, two emails and four text messages all from Claude. The storm within begins to flood his lungs. At least it feels hard to breathe, knowing that he can't get in touch with Gabby and she has not tried to contact him back.

"Okay, what's the game plan?" Winston pulls out the chair beside Josiah and sits down, pen and notepad in hand.

"The solution to everything is not a notepad and pen."

Josiah fires at Winston as the memories of them growing up flash through his mind. One memory in particular paused at the front of his thoughts, the day they were introduced.

> "What's the plan?" Nine year old Winston sits in front of the television blocking Josiah from seeing his favorite after school cartoons.
>
> "We need to write up a plan to stay brothers no matter what."
>
> Remembering this is just who Winston is, Josiah smiles and grabs the pen and notepad from his brother's grip.

After just ten minutes of brainstorming they fill up three pages of notes.

"How is it that I miss my flight and lose my job? Maybe you were right...if I didn't see any signs before, I sure as hell see them now," Josiah confesses before excusing himself from the table.

An hour nap helps to calm his nerves but didn't stop the many thoughts from roaming through his head.

Checking his phone again brings a much needed smile to his otherwise cracked face.

Good evening my love. Sorry just getting back to you. Time difference, you know?

Not bothering to text back, Josiah hits the call button and, to his surprise, he got just what he was hoping for.

"Yes, pickles and oranges... nasty right?" Josiah shares random stories from the last visit to his father's house trying to keep from telling about his failed attempt to surprise her with his relocation to LA.

"Sure can't wait to visit with them again. How is your mother?"

Josiah pauses and not briefly. The silence concerns Gabby.

"Is something wrong," she asks.

She was not there on his last visit to see his father; she was out with friends he had told her. Knowing that she was away, even just for a few hours bothered him. He couldn't help but think she was out doing things she had in her past. He was so consumed with the move and making sure all that was in order he didn't realize he was feeling some kind of way about it.

That feeling then quickly shifts to apologetic. He had planned to tell his father and uncle about the move but didn't think about sharing the news personally with his mother.

"It's fine...she's fine," he stumbles through his words.

Gabby accepts his response for now, making a mental note that she would revisit this topic later.

"My goodness, we've been on the phone for almost three hours," she notices.

Josiah looks up at the wall clock and smiles with pride. He made it that long without telling his secret.

"I better jump off the line. I am really tired."

Josiah looks at the wall clock again. It is just after five in the evening; why is she tired and, more importantly, how did she manage to stay on the phone with no interruptions that long?

"Okay, it's quite early in the afternoon on your side but hey, if you're tired you're tired." Josiah ends the call, not knowing that not only has he kept his secret but Gabby has managed to keep hers.

FINDING OUT

Gabby's decision to hire someone to take her place in LA was not at the top of Victor's list of great things she has done but he was secretly glad to have her back.

"They fear you… make them respect you," he suggested during their first meeting of her arrival back into the office.

LA living lasted just under a year for Gabby but didn't take that long for her to realize she would never consider it home. She allowed work to completely consume her time there as she had no desire to meet and get to know the people of that city.

After placing the finishing touches on the 15th floor, which is her entire office, she sits to enjoy the view from up high. The moment was just that as the intercom on the wall next to the elevator buzzes.

"May I send your visitor up, hun?"

Newbie, who has graduated from Victor's errand girl to front desk attendant since Gabby left, almost sings through the speaker.

She clearly loves her job, just as bubbly as the day she wished Gabby a happy vacation after knowing her all of never.

"Saundra, is it? Don't refer to me as hun, today or any day. And yes, please send Mona up. I am turning the monitor off now. Will be leaving for the evening here shortly."

Without a response from Saundra, she pushes the off button on the intercom.

"I'll be right there! Is the car in the lot or did you leave it out front," Gabby, searching through her pocketbook for her set of keys, asks once she hears the elevator doors open.

"I don't have access to the lot."

Gabby looks up to find Josiah staring back at her dressed in a black waist length pea coat with a red scarf wrapped around his neck. Black slacks and black dress shoes complete the look and it was doing wonders for Gabby.

Her red lips spread wide across her face.

"What a surprise."

"I'll say," Josiah comes back quickly.

The elevator bell dings and Mona stumbles out clumsily.

"I see meeting at doors is our thing," Josiah greets Mona.

"Only this time, you're in my way," she walks around him in pursuit to Gabby, who is chuckling at the look on Josiah's face.

Mona hands Gabby the files she asked to bring down and the keys to the car.

"It's parked in the lot, sleet is pretty thick tonight."

Gabby takes the files, putting them in the cabinet alongside her glass desk. "Take the car and go home. I am riding with my unexpected guest this evening."

Small talk got them from office to sushi bar in the city.

"After getting off the phone with you earlier this week, I called the LA office where I was told you were no longer working there."

Josiah waits for an excuse.

"You always seem to manage ruining a surprise."

Josiah sits back in the seat and thinks a minute.

"Ok, well, you got me. Believe it or not, I am still surprised."

"It's light in here for a Friday night," he notices as they walk through the not so full parking lot of the sushi bar.

He and Gabby had frequented this place in the 'get to know you' stages of their relationship but haven't been back in some time.

While enjoying their California Rolls, they reminisce on the last few years. Time had flown by while so many life events took place. Neither of them found the time to talk about what was going on lately, realizing they have been just letting things happen.

"It amazes me how we both have dealt with so much without saying much about it to each other but yet the support and love was always there. You know, as though we knew what the other was dealing with," Gabby smiles a sneaky smile.

"Speak for yourself. I had no such love or support. Are we in two different relationships? We should run over to the university to see if they are conducting a study on that and sign up!"

Josiah holds a straight face as long as he could, but soon after Gabby, broke out into laughter.

"Do you know the extremes I would take to be with you?"

Josiah watches Gabby closely for hesitation. To his surprise, there was none.

"Of course I do!"

He removes an envelope from his jacket pocket and places it on the table in front of her.

"I don't think you do."

Gabby opens the envelope to find a one-way airline ticket to Los Angeles. Not ringing a bell, she puts the ticket down and checks the empty envelope once more.

"I don't get it."

Josiah tells his secret to Gabby and enjoys every minute of watching her face change surprised expressions every five seconds.

He shared everything from his indecisiveness to his anger at the airport once he realized he missed his flight.

"All I could think about was being where you were... always," he shared, as he wrapped up his adventure in making his way back to her heart.

"What a coincidence. That's all I was thinking on my way back, as well."

With secrets no longer secrets, Josiah gently kisses Gabby on the forehead before opening the door for her to get into his car.

PLANNING

As Gabby makes her way through the bustle of the crowd she takes the time to enjoy yet another beautiful Christmas in the city. Decorated trees were just as tall, bells ringing just as loud and lights just as bright, if not brighter, even in the sunlight. Snow had yet to fall but the chill of Christmas sparked winter wonderlands in her heart.

"Merry Christmas," Gabby stops to place a donation in the red tin in front of her destination.

Happy that she told everyone to show up by eleven, she smiles as family and friends wander in between a quarter and half after.

Luckily, everyone did their part as requested by Gabby to make this afternoon run smoothly so she didn't need the entire hour she planned to have with them in case of forgetfulness on their part.

Everyone was settled and cozy with their choice of liquid warmth by the time the clock struck noon and, just as she knew he would, Josiah walks in right on time.

The very helpful team at the Center Coffee Shop were at the door to greet him with his large Caramel Macchiato and to escort him to his seat.

Josiah grins widely and is so happy when he sees Gabby standing there he didn't even notice the family and friends they share surrounding her.

"It's time to get this wedding in order." Gabby holds the wedding planning magazines and books up high.

"I know this is you all's wedding, but we got our two cent to add." Josiah's grin grows wider. After his uncle speaks up, he notices everyone else.

"I see a wedding in spring, wedding party of twelve, lilies dressing the reception tables, gold ribbons and Prince as the ring bearer."

Even Gabby's mother and sister, Gina, were able to make it down for the week.

Little did she know, Gina had it all planned out. Little did Gina know, Gabby was overjoyed about it. Although excited, she has accepted that the wedding planning bone never formed in her body.

"Bronze, not Gold; that will be better," Valorie, Josiah's mother, disagrees with Gabby.

After a few minutes of back and forth on Bronze and Gold, Josiah steps in with a solution.

"Mothers of the bride and groom should wear beautiful bronze dresses. The two colors are so close, they can be intertwined throughout the décor."

Josiah approaches his mother with a flower made of cream colored construction paper covered in dried glue and gold sprinkles.

"Maybe you can wear this on my wedding day."

Valorie takes the flower and embraces her son as the tears begin to fall.

"You got the box. See, I never forgot you baby boy."

Gabby watches as forgiveness and newness cover the two.

Three hours and three cups of coffee later Gabby was beyond excited about her wedding day. Plans now in order with the help of the family, all she and Josiah have to do now is show up.

Josiah and Gabby blow kisses and wave goodbyes as everyone disperses into the cold of the afternoon. After a few minutes of small talk, I love you's and thank you's Josiah and Gabby go their separate ways for the day as well.

SUNDAY BLESSINGS

By the third hit of the snooze button on the alarm clock, Josiah is finally ready to remove himself from the uncomforting guest bed in the spare room at Winston and Arin's.

"Hey, I was going to fry an egg," Winston says standing in the open doorway.

"Nah, I gotta get dressed and head out. But, thanks man," Josiah turns down breakfast as he rushes past his brother to the bathroom down the hall.

Unaware of the congestion on this street Sunday morning, Josiah talks to himself to try and remain calm.

There are police directing traffic and families running from corner to corner in a rush to get a good seat by start of service.

"And I thought I was getting here early." He complains as he finally pulls into a parking slot.

"Good morning and welcome." He receives a program before walking into the sanctuary.

Knowing she arrives very early for morning bible study, he skims through the room in search of Gabby's big hair.

Finally spotting her near the center of the middle section he makes his way to her.

"I was wondering if I could join you for church today," Josiah taps Gabby on the shoulder.

Gabby's eyes light up when she turns to find Josiah leaning over the seat next to her.

Pushing the seat down, she welcomes him to join her. Worship service was much different than ever before. Gabby could feel the presence of God not only in the building but in her heart and in their life.

"See, prayer changes things," Gabby's mother leans in to remind her just before the praise team hits the stage.

What quickly went from Sunday dinner to house warming, Gabby was delighted with all that had come after service and with gifts.

"Thank you Ms. Valorie, I know just where to put that," Gabby gleams at the beautiful bronze vase she gifted to her.

"Momma Val, if it's ok with you. I'd like to be called Momma Val."

"Of course," she says as she embraces her future mother in-law.

After most of the guests have gone, Mona joins Gabby in the kitchen to begin cleaning.

Gabby steps back a moment and watches Mona as she moves around the kitchen.

"Is something wrong," Mona asks, noticing Gabby's stare.

"You have changed so much in just this short period of time. You are glowing, Mona."

"I am happy," Mona says, becoming bashful with her cheeks turning red fast.

As the night calms and the house settles, the sound of Gina chasing Prince through the house and her mother singing old hymnals is amplified. It isn't a bother to Gabby. It brings joy to her heart.

She had become so use to being alone in her own world with her own idea of a perfect life that she didn't realize all she was missing out on.

Climbing under the covers, bible in hand, Gabby takes some time with God. She searches through the bible looking for a perfect passage for the evening when she hears her nephew in the next room.

"Don't read to me. Just tell me something out the heart in your head."

Gabby giggles and places the bible on the nightstand next to a picture of her and Josiah.

As she gets down on her knees she never takes her eyes off the picture of her and Josiah. She becomes overwhelmed with emotion. He has made such a difference in her life and she is grateful for the changes their meeting brought about.

"You always know what's best and when it's best..." Gabby begins to talk to God from the heart in her head.

"...I know that with love at the center, everything else around me will be perfect. Thank you, heavenly Father... Amen."

AT THE CENTER OF IT ALL

ABOUT THE AUTHOR

Tierza Groce found her inspiration to write after being introduced to the life and art of the late Maya Angelou at the age of fourteen. She would go on to write many poems and short stories of her own that derived from unfortunate as well as beautiful encounters through adolescence. These remained concealed in several notebooks and diaries out of fear of what others would think of her thoughts, feelings and experiences. Although reluctant to sharing her art, she continued writing; believing that there must be a purpose for all that comes to her to put to paper.

Shortly after graduating high school with honors Tierza became a young mother to a son changing her life's path causing her to focus on the necessities of life…working to keep a roof over their head, food in their tummies and clothes on their backs. By mid-twenties Tierza found herself needing a change of scenery so she leaves Minnesota where she was born and raised to take on a whole new world on the east coast in Maryland where she was able to tap into other hobbies such as youth outreach, interior design and music. A few short years later she ended up on a midnight train…well, more like a midnight U-Haul to Georgia where she now resides pursuing her dream of changing lives through her writing which has become her ministry.

www.TierzaSpeak.com
www.facebook.com/TierzaSpeaks
Twitter: @TierzaSpeaks
Contact: tierzaspeaks@gmail.com

www.ingramcontent.com/pod-product-compliance
Lightning Source LLC
Chambersburg PA
CBHW060944180626
46817CB00004B/1704